7/22

TURN the TIDE

TURN
the
TIDE

By Elaine Dimopoulos

CLARION BOOKS
An Imprint of *HarperCollins*Publishers
Boston   New York

Clarion Books is an imprint of HarperCollins Publishers.

Turn the Tide
Copyright © 2022 by HarperCollins Publishers LLC
All rights reserved. No part of this book may be used or reproduced in any manner
whatsoever without written permission except in the case of brief quotations embodied in
critical articles and reviews. For information address HarperCollins Children's Books,
a division of HarperCollins Publishers, 195 Broadway, New York, NY 10007.
clarionbooks.com

Library of Congress Cataloging-in-Publication Data has been applied for.
ISBN: 978-0-358-53815-8

The text was set in Adobe Jenson Pro.
Cover design by Whitney Leader-Picone
Interior design by Whitney Leader-Picone

Manufactured in the United States of America
1 2022
4500845852

First Edition

For Melati, Isabel, and all the changemakers

FOREWORD

Dear Readers!

Hello, and welcome to the beginning of this journey you are
about to set out on where you will hear the story of a girl,
not so different from us, who took action and made change.
It is an immense pleasure and an honor to be featured in this
novel. As the main character, Mimi, observes, "Change does
not happen if no one stands up" — which rings true for our
own journey and the one you are about to read. My sister
Isabel and I founded the organization Bye Bye Plastic Bags to
eliminate plastic bags on Bali, our home, when we were just
ten and twelve years old. You can be that one person to stand
up for climate activism, to question the status quo, and to
bring about radical positive change.

But it is not always easy, and change definitely won't
happen overnight. Sometimes you may feel like giving up,
forgetting about the goal, or looking the other way. But
remember that this vision of a better world is not a vision you
carry on your own. Remember that surrounding yourself with
like-minded people and peers who support your idea is the
very first step of moving change forward.

Change requires all levels of society. We need you, your
siblings, your parents, your teachers, and your community
elders and leaders. So start today and get ready to be inspired

by the words on these pages and the actions taken by other young activists. Now it is your turn to turn the tide, whether you are in Bali or Florida, whether you go to the Green School or a school like Wilford School, whether you are Melati or Mimi.

We don't have the luxury of time to wait before we take action against plastic pollution! Change starts today, and it starts with YOU! We hope you will find the inspiration and the strength from this book to take your first step in creating change for a better world.

— Melati Wijsen, cofounder, Bye Bye Plastic Bags

FIRST MOVEMENT

TREASURE

July swelters.

My mother doesn't let me
sit on our old couch
in our new house
in sweaty, cross-armed protest

when I live in a place
where I can ride my bike
to the beach.

The shells are different here.
New England's shells were
moodier:
stormy clusters of clams and oysters,
mussels glinting indigo.

Florida has speckled junonia,
golden conchs and whelks,
pink bivalves in wide piles
like flower petals.
My shorts grow damp and sandy
as I obsessively
pocket specimens
to store in a glass vase in my room.

"Look!" I say. "This one is barely chipped."

My parents laugh as they unpack.
"Are there any left on the beach?"
my father jokes.

I text Lee photo after photo.
THE PRETTIEST ONE YET! she writes back.

DISSONANT INTERVAL

We're here because the rent
on my parents' restaurant
back home went up
and the money they were earning
didn't.

When I crept to the bathroom
in the middle of the night,
I saw them
banging away on laptops
at the kitchen table.
"Go to bed. We're fine,"
they told me,
even though the creases in their foreheads
looked as if they'd been carved
with paring knives.

I had to hear the news from my cousin Stephanie,
who lived in Fort Myers,
a city on Florida's Gulf Coast.
I HOPE YOU COME! she texted.

At dinner with my mom,
I held out my phone and asked,
"Come *where?*"

My mom didn't even stop chewing her chicken.
"It's called Wilford Island.
Near Fort Myers.
There's a restaurant there for sale
that Uncle Chris heard about.
We're going to visit
together
to see if we like it."

"The restaurant?
Or the island?"

"Both."

After dinner, instead of beginning
with finger exercises,
I took out Chopin's Prelude in E Minor
and played it slowly,
drawing out each mournful suspension.

My mother put her hands on my shoulders
and kissed my head.
"I've missed that old piece," she said.
"Work on the Haydn, though.
Mrs. Krasnova says
it needs to
dance more."

VACATION HOME

Before we moved,
we visited my cousins in Florida
every other year.

After puffy-coating
through a Massachusetts winter,
I always marveled
at the miracle of heat
as the airport doors slid open.

When we visited this time,
we swapped a soggy spring day
for a balmy one.
We drove out of Fort Myers
and soared over an arced bridge called
a causeway.
Two pelicans,
startlingly large,
skimmed the water below us.

Wilford Island,
we discovered,
was oblong,
with one main road running its length.
Smaller roads and driveways

branched to houses and beachfront hotels
hidden behind thickets of trees.
Here and there, tropical flowers
speckled the greenery like jewels.
On nearby paths,
retired couples rode bicycles
in slow motion.

What was it like
to live in a place that felt like vacation
all year long?

THE FUTURE HOME OF THE TRIDENT RESTAURANT

We stopped at a twenty-four-table
Italian restaurant
in the town center.
It was about the size
of my parents' restaurant at home
but with parking.

"*Very* popular," said the retiring owners.
"The tourists have fish for a few days
and suddenly they start craving
spaghetti and meatballs."

Dad said that adding
some pasta dishes to the menu,
along with the souvlaki and spanakopita,
wasn't a bad idea.

We ate at one of the long booths.
The food was okay — a little oily.
My uncle and aunt and cousins all joined us
and devoured the garlic bread and olives.
Stephanie celebrated as if we'd already moved.

"So?" my parents asked me.
"Sunshine and family.

7

We found a piano teacher in Fort Myers.

We promise Lee can visit.

Are you excited?"

WHAT I'D LEAVE BEHIND

Lee Huang and I are best friends
because in third grade
Monique Miranda snuck in at recess
and drew a picture of a walrus
with a big mustache
on the chalkboard
and wrote
Mrs. Breen's name underneath.

Mrs. Breen thought Teddy
had drawn it,
because earlier she'd sent him
to the principal
for accidentally cursing.

I spied the chalk dust on
Monique's fingers
and the mean smile on her face.
I stood up next to my desk
and told Mrs. Breen
that Teddy was innocent
and I knew who did it
but I wouldn't tell.

Lee stood up.
"I know who it is too,
and I won't tell either."

We nodded at each other
and tried not to look at Monique.

Mrs. Breen kept us in for recess,
and Lee and I discovered
we had the same piano teacher
and liked growing things
and were a tiny bit afraid of dogs.

That weekend,
Lee came over
to pick some mums
from our community garden plot.

The following spring,
we tied string bean and tomato plants
to stakes in the garden,

and played the last two pieces
in Mrs. Krasnova's student recital,

and cuddled Lee's new kitten.

PERSPECTIVE SHIFT

No place is perfect.

I'd miss Lee like crazy.

I'd miss watching snowflakes
gust in silent fury
from my living room window
on snow days.
I'd miss the noisy, cozy
radiator in my bedroom.
I'd even miss the grouchy neighbors downstairs,
who banged on their ceiling
if I practiced after eight p.m.

I'd miss seeing Mrs. Krasnova's stern face
beam
when I mastered a tricky section
of Brahms or Mozart.

I'd miss tending our garden,
but Lee's goodbye present
was a new trowel
and daisy-printed gardening gloves.

I wouldn't miss my parents looking pale
and ignoring my questions.

I liked seeing my parents smiling
and talking about the way
the orange trees
and unruly grapevines
reminded them of Greece,
where all four of my grandparents were born.

If I thought of it as an adventure
and if I refused to stomp and sulk
and worry,
maybe the missing wouldn't hurt so much.

MOVING DAY

The day we arrived for good,
the movers rolled my piano
into the living room,
and I made up my bed
in a room that smelled strange.

MY NEW ADDRESS DOESN'T HAVE
AN APARTMENT NUMBER

Our house is light green,
with crunched-up shells and stones
for a driveway.
Inside, white walls touch
tiled hallways.
In the bedrooms,
I walk on spongy carpet.
"Very Florida," my mom says.

It's just a single floor,
but it's a whole
stand-alone
house with a yard.

I can play piano at midnight
if I want
(and if my parents let me).

When my bedroom feels too "Florida"
and I'm tired of unpacking,
I can pedal to a beach
with rosy shells and white sand
that stretches like taffy
in both directions.

GHOSTS IN TREES

I'm filling my pockets.
Tomorrow I start school
(so early here — August 5th!)
and my morning beach visits end.
My prize today: a sand dollar
bigger than my palm.

I find it far down the beach,
where something else catches my eye,
Something mottled and ugly.
I hurry over
and stare.
Plastic bottles and Styrofoam pieces
mark the high-tide line
along with other bits of sea-tossed trash.
My thoughts grow quiet —
then uneasy.

Farther up, near the grasses,
torn pieces of white plastic
snarl around the branches of a short, prickly tree.
They flutter in the shore breezes
like Halloween ghosts.

DISQUIET

I drop the sand dollar,
reach high,
and untangle the plastic.
I shove it into my pockets
and ride home.

I return with my mother in our car,
even though she was in the middle
of trimming cabinet liners
and didn't see how
what I'd found qualified as
"an emergency, exactly."
We bag the trash.
At home, we sort
the recyclables.

"It's done," she says.
"You did a good thing."
She picks up the liners —
then glances at her watch, sighs,
and heads out to meet my dad
at the restaurant.

I don't go with her.
My fingers itch.

Although the piano is in
bad need of tuning,
I pound the left hand
of Emerson's Toccata con Fuoco concerto,
a barreling locomotive,
until lunch.

WILFORD SCHOOL, FIRST IMPRESSION

The building is a single story,
beige, with trim the shade of blue
I think is called azure.

I have nothing to be nervous about.

I already know one of the
thirty-three kids in my grade:
Harper Smith,
my host student,
who plays tennis and has straight hair
that looks as if it's never been cut.
We met up for ice cream at Geppetto's
a week ago.
"Everyone's super chill," she said
as she licked her salted caramel scoop.
"You'll love it."

Now she links her arm through mine
and walks me around outside,
where the seventh-graders are hanging out.
The light touch of her skin
steadies my hammering heart.

She introduces me to everyone.

There are palm trees at my school.
A couple of boys are cute.
It's not so bad.
Everything is clean and bright,

not like my old school,
with its scuffed hallways
and repainted lockers,

and Lee shouting in my direction
over the din of arriving students

and threading a flower in my locker vent
sometimes
as a surprise.

HERE WE GO, AGAIN

When Ms. Miller, our homeroom teacher,
reads my name aloud,
I correct her.

"It's Mimi, please."

MY NAME IS NOT MIMI

It's an easy nickname,
happy and peppy,
but with an edge of sophistication.

It could be
the name of one of Barbie's friends.

I like it —

two solfège notes
even and sure sounding.

My parents planned on calling me Mimi
before I was born.
They claim it was my first word, too . . .

though maybe I was just a selfish child!

MY NAME IS NOT DEMETER

Back home,
my real name was merely unusual
until my class studied Greek mythology in fifth grade.

They called me Mimi
but had seen the other name
on class lists.

In the space of one lesson
I became an Olympian.
Goddess of the harvest.
Earth Mother,
with a daughter who got dragged to the underworld.
Strangely, I took my revenge on humans
in the form of a massive drought
instead of punishing the god responsible.

"... except you spell it weird," my friends said.

Demetra. That's my name.
It's spelled the way it's written in modern Greek,
not ancient.
When my parents say it,
the *D* is a buzzing *T-h*

and they punch the first syllable
(especially when they're annoyed).

Yes, my name is linked
to those stories
of grains and pomegranate seeds,
of famine and bounty.
But I'm short, not stately,
with thick brown hair
that puffs in the Florida heat
instead of cascading in divine waves.
I don't dwell on my namesake goddess . . .

but there are times when I think it would be cool
to dry up a whole field
just because I felt mad.

FIRST DAY

None of the seventh-graders
at Wilford School says anything
when Ms. Miller says my real name.

My first day is fine.
Harper invites me
to sit with her friends at lunch:
Caroline, Grace, Zoe, and Skylar.
They ask me what I'm into
and I say piano
and then the conversation moves on.
They weren't being mean.
It was just that nobody else played,
I guess.

Maybe I should have said gardening?

UPROOTED

Loulouthi mou
is what my father calls me sometimes.
My flower.
Before we left,
he promised
to reserve an area of our new yard
for a year-round garden.

My mom used to say
that my dad believed
if he wasn't at our old restaurant
every minute it was open,
it would sputter and stall and sink
like a motorboat
that ran out of fuel
in the middle of the ocean.

(I don't ask him how it feels
that he was there all the time
and it still stalled.)

But on warm Sunday mornings
back home,
Dad and I would walk
to the community garden.

We weeded and deadheaded,
picked ripe vegetables,
and cut flowers
for our kitchen table vase.

He talked about
how gratifying it is
to grow things,
and how important it is, too.
"Food doesn't just
appear on the table magically," he'd say
as he knelt in the dirt
in stained khakis.
"We Laskarises know
it takes work and passion."

Those mornings never felt like work.
Dad would hum rock songs
and buy me a glazed doughnut
on the way home.
I'd eat it with dirty fingers.

Since we moved,
I've barely seen him.
Four Sundays have come and gone
and he hasn't set up the garden beds
in our backyard yet.

But he's busy,
and he promised,
so I'll wait.

SECOND DAY

Ms. Miller teaches science,
and it might be my favorite class
because she's one of those teachers
with laughing eyes
and a loud voice
who can make even
ecosystem classification
exciting.

THIRD DAY

I put up my hand in science
and ask to get a drink from the bubbler.
A beat of silence —
and then the entire class
bursts out laughing.
I don't know what's funny.
I look to Harper for help
but she's shaking with giggles
and looking at me in amused confusion.

A girl named Carmen Alvarez-Hill is smiling,
but not laughing.
"It's what they call water fountains
in Massachusetts."
She shrugs. "That's all."

"Of course you may, Mimi,"
says Ms. Miller,
and I practically knock my desk over
hurrying out of the classroom.

FOURTH DAY

On the fourth day,
while I'm standing behind Harper,
she invites Grace over after school.
Harper doesn't see me.
When she turns,
and there I am,
she and Grace look at each other.
"Mimi, you should come too," Harper says.

"That's okay," I say. "I have to practice."

Later, Lee doesn't
let me whine.
AWKWARD.
BUT YOU CAN'T BLAME THEM.
IMAGINE THEY'RE US —
THEY'VE BEEN FRIENDS FOREVER.
AND THEY DID INVITE YOU!

I stare at my shells.
I imagine dumping them on the floor,
crushing them under my heels
so their fragments lodge in the carpet fibers.
I imagine stomping into the living room
and telling my parents I want to go home.

Instead, I play a Kabalevsky study,
Etude, op. 27, no. 3,
whose runs zig and zag up and down
like mean eyebrows.

SIGNIFICANT PEOPLE

Two weeks into school,
Ms. Miller lowers the lights
and pulls down the projection screen.

Everyone relaxes. A movie,
good or bad,
is a break.

I watch two sisters,
Melati and Isabel,
stand in the bottom of a bowl-shaped auditorium
and tell their story.

They're wearing faded jeans
and T-shirts printed with the logo
of the organization
they started.

They show the audience a picture
of plastic garbage
on a beach
in Bali,
the Indonesian island
where they live.

I remember the ghosts
from the Wilford beach.
In the dark classroom,
something inside me stirs.

Melati and Isabel
talk about wanting to be
the kinds of
significant people
they've learned about in school.

Bye Bye Plastic Bags.
That's what they call
their campaign.
They educated their community
and organized beach cleanups
and collected signatures at the international airport
and made the governor of Bali
sign an order
to eliminate
single-use
plastic bags.

"Make that difference,"
Isabel says at the end.
"We're not telling you

it's going to be easy.
We're telling you
it's going to be worth it."

MELATI AND ME

As Ms. Miller heads
toward the light switch,
I think many thoughts
in a few seconds
in the dark.

Melati was twelve years old
when she founded
Bye Bye Plastic Bags.

I'm twelve.

She lives on an island.

I live on an island —
without a garden,
or a best friend,
or anything
significant
to do besides practicing piano.

Melati mentioned other places
that have restricted plastic bags:
Hawaii and Rwanda,
Oakland and Dublin.

Why not Wilford Island?

CHANGE DOESN'T HAPPEN IF NO ONE STANDS UP

Isabel wasn't kidding.

It's not easy to speak
in a room full of new classmates
who look and act
as if they're cousins in a big family.

Sitting quietly is safer
when you're not yet sure they're going to
adopt you.

But I remember the way
Lee and I stood up for Teddy.

I think this is a standing moment,
so I rise.

"Ms. Miller," I say,
"if they did that there,
why don't we try
to get rid of plastic bags
here?"

THE BEST SCHOOL ON EARTH

Wilford School is not Green School, Bali.

"We go to the best school on earth,"
Melati said to her audience
in the auditorium.
"We are taught to become leaders of today."

The sisters said
Jane Goodall visited their school.
So did Ban Ki-moon
when he was secretary-general of the United Nations.

I wonder about the most important person
ever to visit Wilford School.
I have not-nice thoughts in my head.
Some bird-watcher.
The weather reporter from Fort Myers.

For kids to make a change,
I wonder if they need
the best school on earth to support them.

But when I look at Ms. Miller's face
shining at me as I stand by my desk,
I think I might be wrong.

Teachers become teachers to inspire kids,
to support their crazy ideas,
at every school on earth.

FIRST STEP

No one stands with me.

Ms. Miller gives it a moment,
perhaps hoping, as I am,
that Melati and Isabel
have stirred something
in another seventh-grader, too.
After all, Melati told her audience,
"Lesson number one:
You cannot do it all by yourself."

"Mimi," Ms. Miller says at last,
"if you and your classmates
want to bring awareness to this cause,
I would love to help you.
As you just saw,
environmental activists
are young and old
and everything in between."

I slide back into my seat.

"Some U.S. cities and states
are passing laws
to ban single-use plastic bags.

The problem is that
about a third of states
have passed
preemption laws" —

she writes it on the board,
her ponytail bobbing —

"so that local governments
can't regulate plastics.
In other words,
these laws ban
any kind of ban.

"And Florida is
one of those states.

"This week, in fact,
to avoid lawsuits,
Surfside, Palm Beach, and Gainesville
repealed plastic bag bans they'd passed."

My mouth twists,
but Melati and Isabel's passion
is still setting off sparks
inside me.

"The Wijsen sisters started with research."
Ms. Miller retracts the projection screen
with a snap.
"Come back and tell us
what you find.
If others want to help Mimi,
please do!"

CRAZY OBSESSED

At lunch,
Harper and the other girls
say that plastic litter is gross and sad
and the sisters in the video were
crazy obsessed with cleaning up their island.
It's supposed to be a compliment, I think.
Everyone's sort of meeting my eye,
sort of not.

They switch
to gossiping about some cute eighth-grader
whom Ethan Hoffman, a different eighth-grader,
interviewed on his podcast,
and how the cute eighth-grader
said something vague about liking a seventh-grader . . .
I don't know what they're talking about,
and I don't really care,

but I ask them about it
and giggle
just to show them
I'm not the new crazy-obsessed girl.

FIRST STOP

After school, alone,
I ride to Frank's,
the supermarket and general store
on the island.

It's bustling,
and I walk my bike through
the parking lot.
("Tourists don't always know
where they're going,"
my dad has warned me.)

At the cashier station,
I see plastic bags only.

At the customer service desk,
I want to ask for the manager
but I'm nervous.
I text Lee for courage.
She doesn't answer.
She's probably practicing —
which is what I should be doing.

I forget about the manager
and ask the woman behind the desk

whether Frank's has
any other kind
of grocery bags.
My voice sounds squeaky,
and she looks at me funny.

"We have
some freezer bags for ice cream
and boxes for wine.
What are you looking for?"

"Any paper bags?" I ask.

"We sell paper lunch bags,"
she answers. "Aisle nineteen."

"And — is there a place
to recycle plastic bags?" I ask,
even though she's already looking
at the next person in line.

"Not on the island.
Can I help you, sir?"

SECOND THROUGH SEVENTH STOPS

On the way home
I stop at three of the tourist shops
that sell T-shirts, ornaments, shells, and mugs.
Then I swing by a beach gear shop,
the coffee shop,
and one of the clothing boutiques.
I ask to see what bags they use
for customers.

Every single employee
holds up a plastic bag.

Most of them look at me
like I'm rude for asking.

DISTRACTIONS

When I finally get home,
I force myself to
do my homework and practice.

While I'm trying
to steady the tempo
on my Czerny studies,
Google search terms
flash in my head:

> Bye Bye Plastic Bags
> Wijsen sisters today
> single-use plastic bags, environmental impact
> single-use plastic bags, Wilford Island
> preemption laws, Florida
> student environmental movements

The Czerny is a mess,
but my mother doesn't say anything.
I'm not sure she notices.

The Trident Restaurant's soft opening
begins in a week.
Mom is printing and
reprinting the menu as it changes,

interviewing serving staff,
and transforming the green and red decor
to blue and white.

My dad all but sleeps at the restaurant.

My parents are stressed, but I can tell
it's the kind of stress that has
a lot of hope mixed in.
I've seen the other kind.

The good news:
Our fridge is stocked with
trial moussaka and pastitsio,
hearty casseroles that taste the way they did
at our restaurant back home.
Which is to say, delicious.

After dinner,
my legs are tired from pedaling everywhere,
and I haven't finished my English assignment,
but I open my laptop,
enter my search terms,
and read articles . . .

until my mother
bangs on my door

and says, "Mimi! What are you
still doing up?"

A GRAINY UNDERWATER PHOTOGRAPH

Under my quilt in the dark,
eyes open,
I think about
the Mariana Trench,
the deepest point in the ocean,
deeper than Mount Everest
is tall.

This year, a man named Victor Vescovo
set a record for the deepest dive
in a submersible.
He spent four hours exploring
the Mariana Trench bottom

and photographed a plastic bag there.

What did that bag carry when it was on land?
Who threw it away?
Where?
How long did it take to drift
down
thirty-six thousand feet
and settle

in a place
few humans
have ever
seen?

THE AGE OF PLASTIC

Plastics I encountered today before 8:30 a.m.
    (an incomplete list):

    my toothbrush handle
    my shampoo bottle
    the bag that holds the cinnamon bread
    the garbage liner
    the barrel of my pen
    the binding on my library book
    the lid of dad's coffee container
    the wrapper of my Jolly Rancher candy
        (which, no, I shouldn't have been sucking
        on the way to school)

The Age of Plastic
is the name of a CD my mom has
in a floppy black collector's case . . .
whose storage-pocket pages are plastic.

Last night I learned
that plastics are cheap and convenient.

Some are reusable
or recyclable,

but some, like grocery bags, are used once
and then thrown away,

washing up on our beaches,
out of sight in our landfills,
silently releasing toxins
wherever they rest.

I can't wrap my brain around
how a human could invent a thing
that could take one thousand years —
one thousand years —
to break up
into microscopic granules
that may never fully
decompose,

bring it into the world,
and sleep peacefully.

IS CARMEN ALVAREZ-HILL REALLY STANDING UP WITH ME?

Carmen Alvarez-Hill
is tall and tan.
Her dark hair falls down her back
in gentle waves
that look natural —
though she must use a curling iron
because no one is that lucky.

She wears woven sandals
with little platforms
in the heels
that make her even taller.

Harper is always
extra friendly to Carmen.
Boys sometimes
turn stupid
when they have to be her partner.
She is the girl in our class
whom everyone wants
to be best friends with
because she doesn't seem to need
a best friend.

This morning,
she is waiting for me
outside the school building.

"Were you serious
about the plastic bag thing?" she asks.
She's wearing gold sunglasses
that make her look like
a pilot.

I try not to
turn stupid.
I refrain from blurting out
the statistics and ideas filling my brain.
"Yeah," I answer.

"Do you want to
talk about it after school?
At my house?"

As my dad would say,
the fates are against me.
"I can't today.
I have a piano lesson —
what about Saturday?"

She nods.
Before she enters
the building, she says,
"Your goddess name
is really cool."

FRIDAY AFTERNOONS

Kyle Chou is my piano teacher now.
This is the second Friday afternoon
we've driven an hour
to his studio in Fort Myers.
(It should be forty-five minutes,
but there's traffic.)

Last week
we arrived early to our first lesson
and he was in child's pose
on a yoga mat on the floor.
It was weird
but kind of nice to know
he practiced something other than piano.

My mother chose him
because his students compete
in juried competitions.
This year, Lee and I will both be eligible
for advanced levels
made up of thirteen- and fourteen-year-olds.
In different states, of course . . .
Maybe that makes it a tiny bit easier
to cheer each other on.

Back home, I qualified to perform at
Carnegie Hall
in third grade but not fourth,
in fifth grade but not sixth.
My parents say I'm due this year.

Lee made it last year for the first time.

It's not what you think:
a packed auditorium rising to its feet
only for you
as you take bow after bow
holding flowers.

The reality:
I waited backstage for nearly two hours
while other children performed,
played my piece,
then waited another hour,
listening to the rest of the kids
from the balcony.
Afterward, we went out for fancy hamburgers.

Nevertheless,
it was exhilarating
to practice so much that my fingers
danced over my quilt in bed at night.

When I sat down at that long Steinway
beneath three crystal-and-gold chandeliers,
nerves stirred in me
but so did pride.
I imagined a time when I might play
with a full orchestra
behind me.

Kyle told me to call him Kyle
instead of Mr. Chou.
"Are you serious about competing?"
he asked me at our first lesson.

"Of course!" I answered.

GIFTED

When I was two,
my parents say I played my first
piano scale.
I don't remember —
but I have a feeling I was just
pressing the white keys
in order
with my index finger.

My mother found out I was
too young for lessons
at the New England Conservatory.
(According to a family story
that makes my dad cackle with laughter,
when she pointed out
that I was gifted,
the director pointed out
that I wasn't potty-trained.)

When I turned five,
my mother got her way,
and I started studying
with Mrs. Krasnova.

FINGER HAMMERS

I remember when
I fell in love with playing.

Mrs. Krasnova was demonstrating
Bach's Prelude in C Major.

From where I stood,
I could see not only
her sturdy fingers on the keys
but also the fuzzy hammers inside the piano
hitting their strings with sureness
and strength.
I listened to her crescendos and decrescendos,
her lively arpeggios,
and her lingering ritardandos.

It clicked.

Piano was more
than precision.
If I first practiced
to get the notes under my fingers,
then I could decide
what the music should sound like.
My fingers could strike

like hammers,
with purpose.
I could enjoy myself.

I didn't say anything
to Mrs. Krasnova,
but at the next lesson,
her lipsticked lips
opened a bit when I played the Bach.

"You were listening," she said.

BESTED

This week
my mind is on plastic bags
and petitions
and what I'm going to wear
to Carmen Alvarez-Hill's house tomorrow.

Kyle has a student before me today,
and in the waiting room
I flip through my music,
looking at fingering,
thinking through
the tricky parts.

The student in with him
is amazing.
I think they're playing Debussy,
and it sounds like a waterfall.

The door opens
and a boy younger than I am
steps out.
He's short, with bangs that hang down
in a straight line on his forehead.

My mother and I look at each other
as he leaves.

I have some serious practicing to do.

SATURDAY MORNING WITH CARMEN AND HER MOTHER

Carmen Alvarez-Hill is *rich*.

I do not think "very Florida"
when I kick off my sandals
and walk barefoot
across her tiled entryway.

I think "very large."

In the hall,
there's a photo of Carmen parasailing.
Another of her
and an older version of her —
her sister, I'm guessing —
with an actor from a Nickelodeon show
whose real name I don't know.

We end up in an open space
that's sort of a kitchen and living room together.
There are glass doors and a deck beyond
that overlooks a piece of private beach
and glittering Gulf waters.

I say hello
to a woman in the kitchen
preparing us chopped vegetables and hummus.

I think that's Carmen's mother
until her real mother walks in
wearing a colorful sundress that goes
all the way to the floor.

She is glamorous
and so happy to meet me.
She carries the snacks to the glass table,
apparently eager to join
our conversation.

THE GREEK MYTH OF ARION AND THE DOLPHINS LEAPS TO MY MIND

"Carmen is passionate about animals,"
her mother says passionately.

Most kids I know
would roll their eyes,
but Carmen smiles at her mother.

They have the same goddess hair.

"Last year, a starving dolphin washed up
on a Fort Myers beach," Carmen says.
"It had two plastic bags
and a balloon
in its stomach.
How messed up is that?"

"Carmen and her sister swim with dolphins,"
her mother says
before I can respond.
"Wild encounters only," Carmen adds,
her eyes serious.

I'm not sure what this means.

She doesn't . . . ride the dolphins,
does she?
Like Arion,
whom my mother says dolphins carried to safety
because he was such a good musician,
so go practice, Mimi — it could save your life!

No, that would be ridiculous.

Still, I can't help thinking
I'm sitting across from
some kind of rich mermaid.

"I read that by 2050,
pound for pound,
there could be as much plastic as fish
in the oceans," I say at last.

Ms. Alvarez shakes her head.
"How sad."

I push on. "I have some ideas about
how we might
start getting the word out
on the island."

"I have an idea too," says Carmen.
"Ma, we're going to hang out outside, okay?"

As she leaves us,
Ms. Alvarez squeezes my shoulder.
She kisses Carmen's forehead
and, with two soft flicks of her thumb,
rubs away the pink smudge that lingers.

STEALING FROM MELATI AND ISABEL'S PLAYBOOK

The lounge chairs on the deck
have wooden frames
and thick sky-blue cushions.

I go first.

My ideas:
We start our own movement
to make Wilford Island plastic bag–free
with a website
and social media accounts.

We ask Ms. Miller
to help us visit each grade at Wilford School
and talk to them
about the harm single-use plastics cause.
We send them home with information
for their parents.

Also, we create a petition.
We ask people to sign
if they support island businesses
no longer bagging their goods in plastic.

The preemption laws might mean
the town council can't pass an official ban,
but education
and a petition
and a social media campaign
could pressure businesses to stock compostable bags
and teach islanders to carry reusables.

Melati and Isabel collected signatures
near customs at the Bali airport.
They got one thousand signatures
in an hour and a half.
But there's no airport on our island.

I tell Carmen I think we should get the signatures
at Frank's.
Most of the seven thousand three hundred
Wilford Islanders
must get groceries
at least once a week, I reason.

I hope I'm not sounding too
bossy
and turning Carmen off.

THE HILL IN ALVAREZ-HILL

A smile twitches across Carmen's face.
"I think we should start with Frank's too," she says.
"My dad owns the store."

She lets this nugget sink in.
I feel so stupid.
I'm not sure exactly how I was supposed
to figure out who her dad was,
but I'm pretty sure
a less stupid person
would have.

"Let's see if he'll stop bagging with plastic."
She crosses her legs
and dips a carrot stick in hummus.
"If he does it,
I bet everyone on the island will follow."

Isabel said making a difference
wouldn't be easy.
But maybe in some cases . . .
it is?

ANOTHER STANDING MOMENT

Mr. Hill will be home from work later,
and Carmen invites me to stay

and borrow a lime-green bikini,
a life jacket,
and sunscreen,
and go paddleboarding.

We wade into the calm water.
I manage to stand up on the board
on my first try.
It's easier to balance
than it looks.

I love the way
I can stare straight down
at the shadows and shapes
on the sea.

Carmen says it's a good core workout.
Her mother waves
from the deck.

"Oh, flip your paddle around,"
Carmen tells me.

"Don't worry —
I didn't know I was holding it backward
until an instructor
corrected my sister and me
when we were in Maui.
Isn't it fun?
Like walking on the water, right?"

Lee isn't a
"when-we-were-in-Maui"
kind of friend,

but I'm keeping an open mind.

HERE'S THE THING ABOUT WILFORD ISLANDERS

I didn't expect
to be pitching our idea
to Frank Hill
wrapped in a beach towel.

We're on the deck lounge chairs.
Ms. Alvarez leans against the doorframe.
Mr. Hill is a little older than his wife.
He has a closely shorn
silvery-gray beard.

"I couldn't agree more,"
he says after listening to Carmen
talk about how plastics are "the worst"
for sea life,

after listening to me describe
how such a small change
in his store
could ensure that fewer ghosts
(except I don't call them that)
tangle in tree branches.

"But here's the thing, girls," he says.
"It's your generation

that's open to this kind of change.
Tourists and year-rounders
want the same Frank's
that's served them for years.
Some are on fixed incomes.
They come to Wilford Island
for consistency.
An easy retirement.
We went to a new ordering system
in the deli
and they practically broke down
my poor manager's
office door."

He chuckles. Carmen smiles.
I don't smile.
We're supposed to back off
because a little change
riles people up?

"What if both kinds
of bags are there," Carmen says,
"and the baggers offer customers
paper first?"

I speak quickly
before Mr. Hill accepts this

watery
compromise.

"The best thing would be
if plastic bags
weren't even available
and if people brought
their own
reusable bags.
The organization
Bye Bye Plastic Bags
sells nylon bags on their website.
Would you consider
selling them in your store?"

TOO GOOD TO REFUSE

Mr. Hill threads his fingers together
as he leans forward
and says he has a better idea.

He wants to sell nylon bags
printed with the Frank's logo.

"Heck, I'll even donate
the first two hundred bags.
You girls can hand them out
for free!"

Carmen beams at her father,
then turns her happy eyes
toward me.

It's a generous offer.

I wonder how long
it took Melati and Isabel
to perfect
the art
of the compromise.

"That would be amazing."
I make my voice sound like sunshine.
"Do you mind if Carmen and I
collect signatures for our petition
against plastic bags
at the same time?"

Ms. Alvarez glides forward
and rests her hand lightly
on her husband's shoulder.

"Go right ahead," Mr. Hill replies.

VICTORY PRACTICE

My finger hammers strike the keys
on my piano
vivacissimo
but with metronomic
precision.

B major scales, my favorite —
F-sharp major, E harmonic minor.
My two-octave runs sound as light
as I feel.

Fingers warm,
I FaceTime Lee
and prop the phone
so we can play for each other.

In her Bach prelude
two wise birds chatter.
I make my Haydn sonata
vault and twirl.

After we gush over each other's playing,
I tell Lee that I have
a new project
and someone to help me —

not yet a friend,
but there's potential.

"Of course you do," she answers,
crossing her legs on the piano bench.
"Tell me everything."

SIGNIFICANT LUNCH: A DAYDREAM

My parents would help me
prepare the meal.
Not a lamb roast with lemony potatoes
this time.

A little bit of everything:
vegetarian, vegan, halal, kosher,
gluten-free, lactose-free, nut-free,
spicy, mild,
green, red, brown, white
dishes.

The table is circular,
set for six.
On my left,
Melati and Isabel Wijsen smile easily
and talk about what it's been like
to take Bye Bye Plastic Bags
global.
I ask questions shyly —
mostly listen.

On my right:
"Water Warrior" Autumn Peltier.

She told the prime minister of Canada
she was unhappy with his choice
to expand oil pipelines
and pleaded with him to protect
the water supply.

Next to her:
Isra Hirsi,
cofounder of the U.S. Youth Climate Strike.
She and Autumn are having
side conversations about
clean water,
human rights,
and how more
young faces in the environmental movement
need to look like theirs.

Halfway through the meal,
when we're talking like old friends and
unapologetically
sharing our appetites
for activism,
the last guest slides into her chair —
late, because she's so busy.

It's Greta, of course.

Greta Thunberg,
who left the ninth grade to hold
a handmade sign —
SCHOOL STRIKE FOR CLIMATE —
outside the Swedish Parliament
alone.

She showed us
how outraged —
how *crazy obsessed* —
we should be about environmental degradation

and how young people
can be so very, very
significant.

SIGNIFICANT FEARS

The lonely quiet of night
is different from
the promising quiet of day.

In the dark,
my daydream
embarrasses me.

I texted Carmen to thank her
for a fun afternoon
but never heard back.
I sent a second text,
a photo of a woman paddleboarding
in sparkly boots and a rainbow wig.
I spent a long time
picking just the right
funny picture.

She sent
a laughing Tapback.
Something.
Not really an invitation
to keep talking.
HA HA.

I miss Lee so much.

On Wilford Island
I have to make up famous friends
who share my interests,
because it's not yet clear
whether I'll have any real ones.

SECOND MOVEMENT

A SIGN

The Dusty Jacket
is a bookstore in a plaza
on Main Street
with a little steeple
and a red awning that
flaps in the breeze.

I visit on Sunday
to see if they have
The Pleasures of Piano Performance
by R. Josefowitz.
Kyle showed me his own tattered copy
when he assigned it.
It's a book with words,
not notes.

It's very thick.

My parents told me
to check here before ordering . . .
Locals supporting locals,
and all that.

Contrary to its name,
the store is clean and airy.

The windows aren't large,
but sunlight spills in through every pane.
A few people stand around,
quietly flipping through books
on the bleached-wood display tables.

At the register,
a tall man with a white goatee
and dark-framed glasses
is working on a computer.

I clear my throat
to ask about the piano book
when my eye catches a sign
hanging from the counter.

Large blue letters spell out

SAVE THE PLANET:
CARRY YOUR BOOKS HOME
IN YOUR OWN BAG!

RALLY

When the man at the register
looks up from his screen
and tosses me a lighthearted
"May I help you?"

I return his serve
with a mighty ground stroke.

"That sign. I love it.
All the other stores around here
bag with plastic. I'm trying to make
Wilford Island plastic bag–free
with another girl from my class.
We're going to get Frank's to sell reusables.
We're starting a petition, too.
Have you heard of Bye Bye Plastic Bags?
Or the preemption laws in Florida?
Wait —"

I hear the frenzy of my words and
stutter step to slow myself.

"Did you even make that sign?"

BENEVOLENT BOOKSELLER

I am relieved
when the man doesn't snort
or smirk
or regard me with
the polite indulgence of Mr. Hill.

He turns,
opens a door near the register.
I see a rising wooden staircase.
"Anne!" he calls. "You are needed!

"I love the sign too," he tells me.
His voice resonates in the quiet bookstore.
"But I didn't make it.
My wife did."

THE DUSTY JACKET'S CO-OWNERS

The sign maker's name
is Anne Lowell.
She has white-gray hair
and wears leggings speckled
with the neon colors of reef fish.

Her husband at the register is Henry Lowell,
who used to teach high school
in Connecticut.
Anne served in town government
before moving to Wilford Island.

Like Kyle,
they tell me to call them Anne and Henry.
They're older, so it's weirder.

Anne actually hugs me when they learn
I'm a New England transplant too.

They ask me to "say more"
about my initiative.

Henry holds up the recycled paper bags
stored under the register.
They give customers used cardboard boxes

for larger purchases.
There are no plastic bags in their store!

Their sign isn't a joke.
They think single-use plastics
are a serious problem.

They have an idea,

and then I have an idea.

MANY HANDS

The Lowells organize
beach cleanups on Wilford Island.
The next one is in December.
They are members of the island's
wildlife refuge.
They mainly get volunteers for the cleanups
from the refuge's email list.

"Sign up!" they say. "You should come!"

I've been to the refuge once.
There's a butterfly house
and a nature center with exhibits
and trails.
My mom and I stayed for a talk
on eagle behavior.

I remember the people there that day
and try to ask my next question
delicately.
"Are the wildlife refuge members mostly
senior citizens?"

"Oh, sure, we're all old," says Anne.
"But don't let that stop you!" says Henry.

"I won't. And what if I could get the kids
at Wilford School to come to the cleanup?"
I don't know for certain
that I can —
but I'm going to talk to them all, anyway.
"We could clean
and spread awareness about plastics
and get signatures for my petition
at the same time."

Henry and Anne look at each other.

"I've been waiting for a seat to open up
on the Wilford Island Town Council," says Anne.
"But maybe you should run instead."

INVITATION

Before I leave,
I ask about my book on piano performance.

"An activist musician!" exclaims Henry.
"Joni Mitchell, eat your heart out!"

I don't know who this is,
but when I learn she's a folk singer
who plays the guitar,
I think Henry is barking up the wrong tree.

They don't have R. Josefowitz's book,
but they'll order it for me to pick up.

The last thing I do
is something I'm usually
embarrassed to do.
But not this time.

I place a piece of paper
on the counter.
"The Trident Restaurant is opening in town.
Here's a coupon
for fifty percent off an entrée.
Come if you have a chance!"

PLAYING IT SAFE

I am shy
around Carmen on Monday morning.

Before school, I sit perched
on the ramp railing
with Harper and her crew.
The August sunshine blazes.

Every so often
I squint at Carmen —
serene, as eighth-graders
congeal around her like sea foam.

Grace is kind enough to ask me
how my weekend was.
I tell her I went paddleboarding
for the first time.

What if I brag about Carmen . . .
and she has no intention of
speaking to me
in school?

PUBLIC PARTNERSHIP

Carmen doesn't look my way
until science.

When class ends,
she gusts toward me like a Gulf wind.
"Let's do this," she says,
and rustles me to
Ms. Miller's desk.

Ms. Miller is gulping water from a silver bottle.
Her face is always
red after class.
She moves a lot when she teaches.

When Carmen announces,
"We're joining forces,"
Ms. Miller runs a wrist
over her forehead
and looks at us curiously.

"My dad's going to give away
reusable bags at Frank's.
Tell her about your idea
for the plastic bag petition, Mimi."

"I did some research," I begin.
Our teacher listens with a
dewy-faced grin.

Later, Harper asks me,
"So, this weekend . . .
who'd you go paddleboarding with?"

SAY NO TO PLASTIC BAGS ON WILFORD ISLAND!

Writing a petition
is like tiptoeing through
beached jellyfish.

In study hall,
Ms. Miller helps us choose language
to avoid getting stung
by the preemption laws.
We want to
"discourage"
Wilford Island businesses
from bagging with plastic.
To "encourage"
islanders to bring reusable bags
when they shop.

To me it feels
as if we're not asking for much.
Ms. Miller assures us
that the town council will listen,
and we don't even need
thousands of signatures to get their attention.
Last year,
two people brought forth a petition
to reduce boat speeds

with six hundred signatures
from island residents on it.
It passed.

We check the website
and see that
five hundred
is the requested minimum.

The town council considers
petition-backed proposals
twice annually,
in January and July.
We have just over four months
until our first shot.

At least our petition title has some punch.
Its rhythm clips along
like a well-skipped rock:
Say No to Plastic Bags on Wilford Island!

EMPTY PAGES

As the signature sheets print,
Ms. Miller shows us a site
where we can post our petition online.
She then digs in a hall storage closet
that smells like crayons
and emerges with a brown clipboard.
We fasten a pen to the clip
with masking tape and twine.

"This is how great movements start,"
she says as she secures the pages
and places the clipboard in my hands.

Did Melati and Isabel
also wonder if they'd
ever
fill all those blank lines?

SIGNIFICANT BIRTHDAY

To sign some petitions,
you have to be
old enough to vote.
Others let you sign at sixteen.
You can petition the White House
at thirteen.

Since ours is a student movement
and we're not trying to dismantle the law,
Ms. Miller reasons that elected officials
should take signatures
from people ages thirteen and older
seriously.

Thirteen-year-old Carmen Alvarez-Hill
writes her long name on the first line.
Whitney Miller fills in
the second.

I have to wait five months
to sign my own petition.

IMMODEST ADVICE

Carmen comes over
on Saturday
so we can make our flyers
and get our school speech ready.

We're at my house,
even though,
when I said, "We should get together,"
I was thinking about her house —
and her hummus, her oceanfront deck, her paddleboards.

Afterward, my mom will overdo it a little,
going on about
how *polite and nice* my *new friend* seems!
Carmen doesn't raise eyebrows
at our still-half-full moving boxes
or at our living room,
which is smaller than her front hall
and crowded by the piano.

"I heard you're good," she says,
crossing her legs on our wool couch.
(How did she hear?)
"Will you play something?"

Fresh off my lesson,
I tackle part of Liszt's Consolation no. 6,
a mountain climb of a piece.
Kyle emphasizes
posture and belly breathing
to improve back and wrist
dexterity.
I try to keep his lessons in mind
as I play for Carmen.

"Incredible," is her response.
"You, like, sweat talent, don't you?"

I mumble away the compliment.

"Own it. Too much modesty hurts girls.
That's what my sister says.
She goes to the University of Miami,
and she's right about everything."

BRANDED MOVEMENT

I may sweat musical talent
but Carmen tells me
my design skills need work.

What's wrong with a long, bulleted list
of terrible ways
plastic bags harm the environment?

She takes over at my computer,
and soon our flyers
have a border of miniature earths.
She puts an X next to a plastic bag graphic
and a check next to a tote bag with a carrot on it.
SAY NO TO PLASTIC BAGS
arcs across the top.

It's prettier than bullets,
I'll admit.
Still, the way she just
started changing things
chafes a little —
like sand in my bathing suit.

I tell her about the Lowells
and how we need to announce the beach cleanup
to the kids in each grade.

"Mm-hmm," she says.
She's looking through my window's
bent blinds.
"What's our movement's brand?"
Her fingers, with their pretty, clean nails,
tap my desk.
"Aquatic, right? We're an island.
Keep plastic out of the sea.
Save the marine animals."

There are pauses between my words.
"I don't
know anything about
brands."

"I do."
She opens a new document
and completely redesigns the flyer.

UNINVITED

I still sit with Harper,
Caroline, Grace, Zoe, and Skylar
at lunch.

Carmen hasn't gusted toward me,
the way she did in science,
with a breezy invitation
to join her table.

EUTROPHICATION

The circular-saw-blade teeth
of Hurricane Dorian
sliced at Wilford Island
yesterday.

We followed town orders.
We filled our car with fuel
and stocked a week's worth of water
and nonperishable food.

My dad took down the art we'd just hung,
secured the storm shutters,
and pushed our beds away
from the windows.

The wind
rasped overnight
like a haunted power tool.

We were lucky —
after pummeling the Bahamas,
Dorian swerved and hit
the opposite coast of Florida
and traveled north.

Wilford Island had only to clean up debris
and deal with red algae.

I notice rusty clumps on the shoreline
the next morning.

News reports say
they're caused by "eutrophication" —
excessive nutrients in the water,
churned up by the storm.

They'll wash away, eventually.
They stink like rotting meat.

MORE DORIANS

When school reopens, everyone buzzes
with hurricane stories.

Ms. Miller shows us a chart
with data on how
Gulf hurricanes are getting stronger
and more frequent.

We had hurricanes back home,
but living on a tiny island
at Hurricane Alley's welcome gate
feels more exposed
and terrifying.

"Fossil fuels
are the building blocks of plastic bags,"
Ms. Miller says in a low voice
on my way out.
"Fewer bags
means less oil, gas, and coal extraction,
which burns less carbon,
which makes a positive climate impact."

She gives me a small, pink-cheeked smile.
"You're doing your part, Mimi."

WASTE

I catch my mother
throwing a plastic cereal box liner away
in the kitchen garbage.

"Okay, okay, enough!
I'm sorry!" she yells
after I yell at her
for not washing it out
and putting it in the bag under the sink
that we bring to a grocery store
in Fort Myers
to recycle
every couple of weeks.

"My stress level is up to
here, Demetra!
We're trying to charm
our early customers,
and your father wants to spend
every penny of our loan
on the final design touches —
mostly to impress Uncle Chris,
I really think —
and I don't need my only child
lecturing me!"

I don't speak
as she rinses out the bag
and hangs it like a flag
on a drying rack hook.

Her back relaxes.
"You're not wrong, though."

Without looking at me,
she opens her laptop
and returns to work.

THE LOWELLS VISIT THE TRIDENT RESTAURANT

Anne wore chartreuse.

Henry ordered the kokoretsi
because his waitress said it was
the most adventurous thing on the menu.
He ate every
adventurous bite
of the unmentionable lamb parts.

They stayed through Saturday night closing.
My dad tells me he laughed with them
for half an hour while he wiped tables.
They said they'd met his
"thunderclap of a daughter"
but didn't present my coupon.
He gave them a discount anyway.

They are in my backyard now
because he invited them over
to help plant our new garden beds!

ISLAND GARDEN

"They say you need two green thumbs
to grow vegetables
on Wilford Island, Joni,"
Henry says to me.

"Her name is Mimi,"
my mother interjects, puzzled,
as she pours everyone glasses
of sweetened iced coffee.
Chuckling, Henry explains the reference
to the Joni I remind him of,
who sang about
pesticides and
deforestation.
My father puts a speaker in the window
and plays one of her albums.

Henry goes on.
He ticks the gardening challenges off
on his fingers:
"Transplant shock,
sandy soil,
heat,
pests,
disease."

I am not discouraged.
In our old community plot,
my dad and I coaxed
limp, yellowing tomato plants
into leafy giants flush with fruit.

We plant peppers, spinach, tomatoes.
Eggplant, too —
which usually goes in the ground
earlier in the year,
but which my dad tries anyway
because it's his favorite vegetable.

Anne has brought over some
marigolds and basil.
She calls them a "good bug border,"
drawing bugs that eat pests.

It feels like home
to sink my fingers into soil
instead of sand.
I tear the bottom leaves
off the tomato plants
tenderly,
bury their stalks deep so their roots can spread.
I smile at my father,
who looks tired

but has kept his promise.

I text Lee pictures of the planted beds,
my dirty fingernails,
and a basil leaf on my stuck-out tongue.

She sends me one with her teeth
piercing an apple.
I am momentarily astounded to remember
that back home the air is chilly
and the farm stands smell like cider.

The Lowells wave flailing-armed goodbyes
from their convertible —
then drive back to our house
when they realize
they forgot to give me
my piano performance book.

TAKE PLEASURE

I thought
The Pleasures of Piano Performance
by R. Josefowitz
would be about how to practice
like a maniac
and win competitions.

It's not.

It's about the experience
of mastering a piece of music
and finding pleasure
in performing it for others
and for yourself.

It's right there in the title.

I'm in the middle of a chapter
called "Natural Memorization."
Sometimes seeing a tricky part coming
and reading the notes
makes your heart
pump and your fingers
slip.

Put the score away,
and your attention is fully on
the music you're creating.
I know exactly what R. Josefowitz
means.

I could have written this book!

FIRST WILFORD SCHOOL CLASS VISIT

A few things no one told me . . .

1.
Kindergartners can sit still for
approximately eight minutes
before they start
popping like popcorn.

2.
Words kindergartners don't understand:
    conservation
    decomposition
    toxins
    ban

3.
The story of ocean mammals
swallowing plastics and dying
literally makes them
cry.

Carmen and I creep out of the classroom
as the teachers open their arms
to their students for hugs.

With sniffling as our soundtrack,
we stuff flyers
into the kindergartners' cubbies.

Carmen suggests gently,
"Maybe I'll start us off
in first grade?"

GRADES ONE THROUGH SEVEN

Saying the same thing
over and over with Carmen listening
gets embarrassing.
I try to switch up my lists and statistics
for some variety —
and end up jumbled.

Carmen stands tall when she talks
and gestures with her hands
because she's not holding notes.
She has a no-big-deal-but-it's-a-big-deal
vibe.
Light and heavy.
Likable.

But the Wilford kids are nodding
in the same kind of
big-deal-but-no-big-deal
way.
I wonder how many of them
will rush home and demand
that their parents shop with reusable bags
and sign the petition
and go to the beach cleanup.

"This is important."
My voice is a
teakettle whistle
of urgency.
"We have to do something."

Carmen nods. "Totally."

PODCAST PUBLICITY

I read my speech word for word
to the eighth-graders.
I barely look up at their
high-school-ready faces.

I smell my
pear-scented deodorant
the whole time I talk.

Afterward, when they have taken flyers
and passed around the petition
and are back to talking
about things other than plastic bags,
a boy saunters up to us.
He's exactly my height
and super skinny,
as if he missed school
the day the eighth-grade boys
washed their lunches down
with growth serum.

He knows Carmen, of course.

"Ethan! How's *The Scaled Fish?*"

"Good — better if you both come on
and talk about plastic bags,"
he says with a salesperson's grin.

His name is Ethan Hoffman,
he hosts a podcast that most
of the middle schoolers listen to,
and he can record an interview this weekend
if we "activists" are free.

"I'll be in Miami, visiting Liliana," says Carmen,
"but Mimi can do it."

And I say yes
because despite his smooth talk,
Ethan sounds like the kind of kid
who might not mind someone
with a shrieking teakettle message.

WINNING CONVERSATIONS

On the way to my piano lesson,
I download episodes of
The Scaled Fish.

(Last year, Ethan's voice was higher!)

From the Wilford postmaster,
I learn how trucks, boats, and planes
get mail to the island.

Ms. Miller has a pet iguana
named Smaug
that she's crazy about.

Harper led the tennis team
to an almost undefeated season
last year.

These stories shouldn't be as
interesting as they are.

Ethan asks an unusual question:
"If Smaug could talk, what would he tell you?"

And follows it up with another one:

"What would be the most important thing you'd tell him?"

He's good!

NOCTURNE OP. 15, NO. 1

Kyle and I decide
we're going to prepare
a handful of piano pieces
and pick which ones feel right
for the competition.

I'm most excited about
Chopin's Nocturne in F Major.
Its thunderstorm of a middle
nourishes a gentle meadow by the end.
When Kyle plays it for me,
I imagine the fun
of making my fast notes
pound the dry earth
when the storm hits.

He's not as approving as Carmen
when he hears the Liszt.
My tempo could be more even.

"Review the same section
for next week," he tells me.
Seeing my face, he adds,
"It's okay to take more time!
Liszt is tough."

I wonder if my mom hears.

"What do you think of adding
fifteen minutes to your practices?"
she says on the drive home.

I guess she did.

RUN-ON SENTENCES

Hey Mimi so like I said I want to interview you for the scaled
fish podcast, your getting rid of Plastic Bags idea is really
cool it something I didn't think about much before, I can't
believe people use so many and they could be around for
century's. I usually start with a goal for the podcast, here
it pretty easy, the goal is to get the word out about Plastics
and tell kids to have there parents sign your Petition, so
my questions below are mostly about that, but its also
fun for listeners to learn a little about you so some of the
question are sort of fun and nonrelating. Just let me know
if anything sounds wierd to you but I think it going to be
great!

I have to read
Ethan's email
slowly
and twice.

The easy, articulate interviewer
writes with the grace
of an oily-winged
seabird
trying to fly.

TENDING BEDS

Before I leave for Ethan's,
I water the garden.

The plants aren't bigger,
I don't think,
but they stand firm and
expectant.

I peer closer
and flick
a family reunion of beetles
off the tomato stalks,

then sneak another nibble of basil.

SCALED

Ms. Miller made us all squirm once
by describing how Eurasian otters
disembowel
toads before eating them.

In Ethan's podcast interview,
I feel like the toad.

> "What do you miss most about Massachusetts?"
> "What was your first impression of Wilford Island? Be
>   honest!"
> "How did you become an activist?"
> "Why plastic bags — instead of other environmental
>   causes?"
> "How do you and Carmen plan to change things here?"
> "What's your favorite dish at the Trident Restaurant?"

He sent some of the questions in advance,
but my guts nevertheless feel
as if they're oozing out of my
slashed belly.

Maybe it's because the probing otter
across the table
seems to care about my answers ...

or maybe it's that I want those
petition signatures.

I let myself get turned inside out.

"Ethan," I say,
"have you heard of the Mariana Trench?"

THAT'S A WRAP

Ethan does not live
in a mansion with a maid.
He has a house a little bigger than mine,
with books and bags and sports gear
strewn all over the carpeted floors.
He has two older siblings
and a dog
that I pretend to like.

His interview room
is a small office off the kitchen.
We spoke into microphones.
He "adjusted my levels"
before we began!

Ethan tells me I "killed" the interview.
He's going to edit it today,
and it will "drop" tonight.

On the way home,
I take another chance
and text Carmen.
I tell her
to listen later
for the drop of the podcast.

(After I press SEND,
I wonder if I typed that right.)

This time, she replies.
WILL DO — AND THE BAGS ARRIVED!
GIVEAWAY NEXT WEEKEND?

UNGAINLY GODDESS

On Monday,
Carmen's sitting at our lunch table
when we arrive.

"Mimi, you're unstoppable.
Did you listen to *The Scaled Fish?*"
she asks the other girls,
who mirror her mercurial smile
and prattle that they'll listen, for sure, definitely.

"You heard our presentation,
but Mimi mentioned a gazillion
more ways single-use plastics hurt the environment.
She's totally going to change the world,
like those girls in Ms. Miller's video.
You know she's named after
a goddess, right?"

Her endorsement dazzles like a spotlight.
I want to squint.

While I try to knit my words
into a gauzy response,
Zoe approaches.

Carmen is in her seat, and Zoe's forehead
crumples with questions.
"Should I pull up another chair?
Or ..."

Carmen glances at me,
as if I,
the new girl,
am supposed to weigh in on
friendship rules that precede me
by seven years.
I keep quiet.

"Oh, sit, Zoe. I won't stay."
Carmen gathers her untouched lunch.
"Promise you'll listen, okay?
And get your nylon bags
at Frank's this weekend!"

Everyone's a little giddy after Carmen leaves,
as if they all haven't been
in school with her forever,
as if she's a mermaid with magic glitter dust.
Me,
I'm the landlubber with the lecture:
"A Gazillion Reasons to Boycott Plastic Bags."

Although I'm Carmen's anointed one,
I obsess about what each of the girls
really thinks of me.

She's totally going to change the world, Carmen said.

Why not *We're?*

TWO HUNDRED IS ENOUGH, RIGHT?

After school, I should start practicing,
but I ride to the Dusty Jacket instead
to ask a favor of Anne and Henry.

It's their wildlife refuge email list
I'm after.

"We're giving out free nylon bags
at Frank's on Saturday,"
I explain to Henry at the register.
"Do you think you could let
the refuge members know?
We're collecting signatures
for our petition, too.
It's our first big push."

"You got it, Joni." Henry chuckles earnestly.
"I hope you have enough bags.
If there's one thing Wilford Islanders love,
it's free stuff!"

INVESTED

All week,
my phone is a hornet,
buzzing and needling me
with Carmen's thoughts
about . . .

> the dimensions for the table outside Frank's . . .
> where exactly we should set it up . . .
> what color the tablecloth should be . . .
> whether we should wear clothes in the same color
>   family . . .
> why handmade posters are *not* okay . . .
> how big the printed posters should be . . .
> whether we have time to get buttons made . . .
> or T-shirts . . .

Carmen thinks these things matter
a LOT
because our giveaway
is a chance for a photo op.

"One good photo
can get the whole island invested," she says.

To me,
these decisions take a lot of time
and matter less,
but it feels good to be invested
in a project like this
with someone who
maybe really is invested
in working by my side.

PREPARATION

The day is overcast,
which Carmen says is flattering
for photographs.

Ms. Alvarez is wearing gold sneakers.
We maneuver the folding table
out of her trunk,
cover it with the tablecloth,
and display the glossy posters
and some nylon bags fanned out,
with more bags hidden under the table.
"*That's* why we needed the cloth," says Carmen.

I step back and feel a flutter in my belly.
The money and time Carmen spent
on everything
make us look
like a real organization.
I thank her and her mother
four times.

I don't see Mr. Hill anywhere.

We're ready by 6:45 a.m.
Carmen adjusts her sunglasses

on top of her head
and texts a selfie of us to her sister.
"She won't respond —
she's still asleep," Carmen says.

Ms. Alvarez hangs
a large camera around her neck.

I clutch the petition
and draw a tiny swirl
to double-check that the pen works.

Frank's doors open at seven!

GIVEAWAY

"Say no to plastic bags on Wilford Island!"
It takes guts
to shout at strangers
in the early-morning air.

The first shopper
looks at me with concern
and walks into the store.

"Free reusable Frank's shopping bags!"
Carmen sings out.
Two women approach.

We give them each a bag
and a flyer
and ask if they'd like to see less plastic
on their beautiful island.
They sign our petition!

More shoppers approach.
Crowds draw crowds,
we discover.

Soon we have a little system:
flyers first,

then an appeal to pass on plastic,
then a request to sign the petition,
before we hand over the bags.

Curious shoppers thicken the line
in front of our table,
and many of them say that Henry and Anne sent them,
and a really loud one says, "Girls, I *love* your passion!"
and then Henry and Anne themselves show up
with hugs and more friends,
and Ms. Alvarez is taking a million photos,
and my hair is puffing in the humidity
but I don't care
because it seems that everyone on the island
cares
about getting rid of plastic bags.

Only a few people take bags
without signing the petition.
Plenty of couples
take a single bag between them
and each sign their name.

By noon,
we're out of bags,
and we've collected
two hundred seventy-one signatures.

PARKING LOT PRELUDE

The pages
of blue-inked names
crackle as I flip through them.
The electric sound
is music.

I should know.

A MOM THING

Ms. Alvarez brings us
grilled veggie sandwiches from Frank's
and makes us stop to eat.

I don't want to stop —
every person who goes by
is a lost signature —
but she's persistent in that
it's-not-a-request
mom way.

My mother is busier on weekends
and wears flashy clothing
only to weddings and to my recitals ...
but she makes sure I take time
for meals too.

Carmen tells me she's a vegetarian.
I consider what it would be like
to eat less meat.
I wonder if I could do it
(or if my mom would stand for it).

DIVISION OF LABOR

I peer over Carmen's shoulder
as she flips through her mother's photos
on the camera screen.
She was right —
the table and posters and our faces
pop
against the soft gray light.
Carmen looks pretty and serious.
I look okay . . . and very serious.

"Are you cool with me
being in charge of
our social media accounts?" Carmen says.
"I like branding.
I think I'd be good at it."

She looks at me innocently,
as if she hasn't just grabbed
a major part of our movement
for herself.

"Oh. What would I do, then?"

"Keep collecting signatures in person.
When you talk, people listen.

But we won't be taken seriously
if people can't find us online
and sign the petition that way.
We'll each play to our strengths,
you know?"

What I know
is that I imagined us
both
canvassing the island for signatures
as we did today;
both
curating and managing
our Twitter account
and the rest of it.
Standing or sitting
next to each other.
Like a team,

which, frankly, I thought
I was the captain of.

Ms. Alvarez sits on the curb
with her hands wrapped around her knees,
smiling at us.

I cannot bring myself to tell flawless Carmen
or her flawless mother
that her flawed idea upsets me.

We agree to split responsibilities.
I'll keep approaching shoppers and store owners.
Carmen will crop photos on her phone
and add cute captions
and post her creations.

Carmen places the clipboard in my hands.
"Those signatures will fly in online.
I promise."
She turns to her phone
to call her sister,
who hasn't replied to her text
but should be up by now, she thinks.

"Please thank your dad for the bags," I reply.

INSINCERE

I walk my bike
past the jack-o'-lantern decals on
Frank's storefront windows.
In the parking lot,
I see a cartful of
ghosts —
not the Halloween kind.
The scary kind.

A man in flip-flops
with a crying baby in his cart
is loading groceries
into a station wagon.

Some of his groceries
are in a Frank's nylon bag.
The rest are in
crinkly white plastic bags
with handles.

One plastic bag holds a carton of eggs.
I can tell, by the way
he grips it with both hands
and nestles it

to the side of the groceries
in his trunk.

That single bag,
which will hold eggs for twelve minutes,
could outlive him
by centuries.

Inside my head,
I'm stomping and screaming
and hurling my clipboard to the pavement,

but I decide not to confront this
hypocritical
but tired-looking islander,
who signed our petition.

I'm off to scale bigger fish.

SMALL-BUSINESS SETBACKS

The manager of the first
souvenir shop I enter
refuses to sign my petition.
So does the manager of
the second.

"Don't get me wrong.
I love the environment.
That's why I live here,"
each tells me
in her own words.
But then they talk about
slim profit margins,
small-business fees,
and how, if the state of Florida
wants to pay them the difference
to give away compostable bags,
fine —
but until that happens,
plastic it is.

EVEN CRAZY-OBSESSED PEOPLE HAVE FEELINGS

They're nice enough about it,
but getting turned down
makes me burn with embarrassment.
Outside,
I grip my handlebars
and force swallows
until the tears
filling my eyes like tide pools
dry up.

I don't know
if I wish Carmen were with me
or not.

THE DIRTY TRUTH

Even in different hemispheres,
small island businesses
have things in common.

From my research:

Melati and Isabel made
real change happen on Bali . . .
but not everything is perfect now.

The *South China Morning Post*
reported on a fruit seller named Dini,
who still sells her fruit
in plastic bags,
even after the governor's order.

She explained that
she doesn't have
a big shop in a mall
or a supermarket.
"Let's be real," Dini said.
"They have the money
to give customers free paper bags.
How can fruit sellers like me
give those for free?"

Fruit sellers on Bali
don't face fines.
No one brings Dini to court.
No one has stepped in, either,
to help her with the cost
of alternative bags.

There are fewer plastic bags on Bali now,
but they're still there.

THE DIRTIER TRUTH

I try one more store,
a beach gear shop.

"That's a myth,"
says the guy at the register
whose peach polo shirt
is buttoned all the way up —
who isn't the manager
but gives me his opinion anyway.
"Paper bags take
more resources to produce
than plastic bags.
And I read
that you have to use a reusable bag
twenty thousand times
to make up for the energy spent
to manufacture it.
Your boycott's misguided."

From my research:

Yes,
in production,
paper bags

have four times the carbon footprint
of plastic bags.

No,
you have to reuse most bags
eleven times to improve on a plastic bag,
not twenty thousand.

Yes,
it's not great
to go buy expensive cotton bags
with trendy logos
in the name of the environment . . .
and never use them.

But guess what,
industries interested in selling plastics
use the statistics this guy has seen
to make plastic bags seem like
the best choice.

They shrug
at the postproduction pollution,
the costly waste management,
the dead wildlife,
the human health risks,

the giant patch of garbage
churning in the Pacific Ocean.

Plus, if we change to
carbon-neutral production,
the greenhouse gases from reusables
go way down,
and the benefits go way up.

I am not misguided,
but these fiery arguments in my head
refuse to blowtorch their way out of my mouth
and sear —
er, educate —
this know-it-all.

I'm tired,
and I can't keep talking to clerks and managers
with watery eyes.
I pedal home.

Let's be real:
Making a difference is complicated.

THIRD MOVEMENT

LEE IS COMING!

Since I found out,
I feel as if I have a belly full
of warm avgolemono soup,
with another bowl waiting for me.

Lee, Lee, Lee!

She is flying down
the weekend
after Thanksgiving weekend.

It's the time the "snowbirds,"
with houses up north
and on Wilford Island,
tend to flock south
for a warmer winter.

(It seems like a waste
for a whole house
to stay empty for six months,
doesn't it?)

Because of the influx of islanders,
my parents have scheduled
the Trident Restaurant's

grand opening
for that weekend.
With the final touches complete,
we'll throw a huge party
for as many customers as possible.

And Lee will be there.

I won't have to force a smile
or watch my words
or wonder about loyalty

for forty-eight whole hours.

DELAYED REACTION

Ethan catches me off guard
in the hall
before fifth period.

"Mimi! Did you ever listen?
What did you think?"

I've seen him
since the podcast episode aired.
We've exchanged smiles in the hall,
one thumbs-up.

I find my words
and tell him I thought it was great
even though it was weird
to listen to the sound
of my own voice.
(It got easier
the third and fourth times through,
but I don't tell him this.)

"I did something," he says,
his showman's grin returning.
"I wrote to the paper."

OP-ED

Ethan contacted the *Wilford Islander*
to see if they would be interested
in publishing
an opinion piece
written by some local students
on the environmental harm of plastic bags.

"I thought you, me,
and Carmen could sign it.
Or it could just be from you two,"
he adds quickly.
"I like journalism,
that's all,
so I might be able to help.
And you've convinced me.
There's no reason
Wilford Island shouldn't be
plastic bag–free."

I don't usually experience
bliss
at 1:25 p.m.
on a Tuesday.
But as I imagine my arguments
in newsprint

or on device screens,
convincing an island's worth of readers
to put the earth first,
my head starts to hum.

"I'm so glad you did that!
I have so many ideas for it.
Is there a word limit?
We can worry about that later,
I guess,
when they get back to you.
Let me know when they get back to you!"

"I will. First thing," says Ethan. "Cool."

"Cool. So cool."
I stop there before I say something
uncool.

@WIPLASTICBAGBOYCOTT

Say No to Plastic Bags on Wilford Island
now has a Twitter handle.

I know because Grace —
not Carmen —
showed it to me on her phone one morning.

Almost every Tweet
has a photo attached:

many from the bag giveaway
at Frank's;

some of Carmen on a boat
in a silver bikini
with honest-to-goodness
dolphins in the background;

one of her
in the lime-green bikini I borrowed,
standing in the sand
and holding a dirty plastic bag ghost
with a stick.

Some of the likes and responses
are clearly from friends:
THIS IS A COOL CAUSE!
YUCK! PLASTICS ARE NASTY.

Some responses say nothing about plastic bags
but comment on how she looks,
with kissing or flame
emojis.

I wonder how Carmen feels
reading those.

ONE HUNDRED SIXTY-SIX TO GO

In the Twitter bio
there's a link to our petition.
We have sixty-three signatures online.
When I look closely,
I see the names of some eighth-graders,
who also signed the paper petition.
I'll have to check the lists
against each other.
We want to get to five hundred
fairly.

I wade through the clump
of Carmen's admirers
and hold out my phone.

"We're on Twitter," I say to her,
hoping my tone says,
and were you even going to tell me?

"Yeah! And a bunch
of other platforms, too."
She's grinning,
but there is something strained
in her face.

168

I lower my voice.
"Are the comments
bothering you?"

She waves her hand. "I ignore them."

To get a straight answer
out of this slippery talker,
I muster courage
and ask a direct question.

"Why didn't you tell me
our social media was live?"

"Oh, Mimi, I wanted to surprise you
with a thousand signatures.
It's slower going than I thought,
mainly because we have to get them
from *residents* —
I mean, if we didn't, my sister could get
a thousand with one text —
but I'll get more!
My mother's going to help."

I nod,
slowly taking in

that Carmen Alvarez-Hill
was worried about
disappointing
me.

SOLO SOLICITOR

For the next few weeks
I cut my practice time in half
and ride to Frank's
every day after school.
The jack-o'-lantern decals
have been replaced with cartoon turkeys
and ads for pies.

I stand near the entrance door

without a table,
without a friend,
without posters,

with my clipboard of signatures
and my voice.

I could ask Grace
or Harper or Zoe or Caroline or Skylar
to join me.
Grace might say yes
because she's the nicest.
I don't want a pity *yes*, though,
and I want to hear *no, sorry,* even less.

Standing there,
sometimes I wonder
what brought me so far down this road . . .
The video in class
and the ghosts I saw in the trees,
yes,
and also (a little bit)
the need to keep busy
in an unfamiliar place.

When it gets hard,
I glance at a photo of
Melati and Isabel
on my phone.
(Is that strange?)
I remember the confidence
and urgency
in their voices.

They wanted to be significant people on Bali.
No matter how my activism began,
I know too much now to stop.
To be significant
there *and* here
sometimes means
thrusting flyers at unpleasant strangers

and asking them
to make a small
but significant
change.

MUSIC KIDS GET A'S

Kids who play classical music
have a reputation
for doing well in school.

Mastering a tough piece
and getting good grades
use the same skill set:
discipline, focus . . .
okay, maybe a little perfectionism.

When my reading quiz
comes back
with a 72 on it,
an unfamiliar shame
drenches me like a wave.

We had to match quotations
from *The Wednesday Wars*
with the characters who said them.
I messed one up,
so all the rest got messed up.

Still,
I could have studied more

if I'd come straight home from school
each day this week.

I don't plead my case.
I fold the quiz
into a neat little triangle

and flick it into the recycling bin.

TWO ODDBALLS

In study hall,
Ms. Miller kneels next to my desk
and asks how everything's going.

"You looked a little
blue
in class today," she says.

I raise my eyebrows in feigned
skepticism
and give her the most convincing
"I'm fine!" I have in me.

"You know," she continues,
"I have a pet iguana.
I'm in a roller derby league
in Fort Myers.
Sometimes it's hard living
in a small island community
where not a lot of other people
share your interests.
But I just keep on being me.
And you keep on being you,
you hear me?"

She is trying to be kind —
but seeing how clear it is to my teacher
that I haven't settled in here
makes me feel even more
like a failure.

I redirect.
"I heard you talk about Smaug
on *The Scaled Fish* podcast . . .
but what's roller derby like?"

And I get to listen
while I picture
my mild-mannered science teacher
zooming around a flat track,
hip-checking opponent skaters
and whipping teammates to victory.

LEE IS HERE!

I pick Lee up from the airport
wearing my Allegro Young Artist Competition T-shirt,

and she's wearing hers.
We didn't plan it, I swear!
We laugh and hug and laugh some more.

Lee got a haircut for the trip.
Her sleek, straight hair
that I've always been jealous of
falls in layers
below her chin.
I tell her it looks amazing,
and she says, "So does yours,"
even though my hair is doing its usual
humid puff
and making my neck sweat.

In the car,
with my mom there,
we catch up on her family
and the kids from school we all know.

Lee's mom's migraines have improved.
Teddy is class vice president!

A family called the Johnsons
took over our community garden plot,
and they mostly want to grow
spinach and kale.
They seem okay.
"They're not you, though,"
she says with an exaggerated
downturned-lip frown,
which I return.

NEW DEVELOPMENTS

In my room,
Lee is more interested
in telling me
which seventh-graders like
which other seventh-graders
and who kissed whom and when and how . . .
according to rumors.

In sixth grade,
I was the one with the
sort of half crush
on a boy named Oliver
who seemed quiet and nice.
But it faded when I smiled at him
a few times
and he didn't react.

Lee never liked anybody before.
Now there's some boy
named Michael
who plays soccer
and stands behind her in chorus.
She won't ever do anything
with him, she says,
because she has no time after school

between homework and piano.
Still, she tells me, flushed,
she's thought about kissing him.

She asks me if there's anyone I like.
I remember wondering
about the boys at Wilford School
when I arrived.
I haven't thought about boys
since.

Only petitions
and plastic bags.

CRAZY-OBSESSED UPDATE

Lee wants to do makeovers
like we used to.
She chooses a plum eye shadow for me
that she says is supposed to "contour."
I think it's going to look like a bruise,
but I let her apply it.

As she brushes my lids,
I fill her in
on my campaign:
the awkwardness of the class visits,
the success of the podcast,
the weirdness with Carmen,
the helpfulness of the Lowells,
and the stalled petition.
"I'm obsessed with
getting rid of single-use plastics
on this island."
It feels GREAT to say it out loud.
"It's the good kind of obsessed,
you know?"

Lee nods, and I start in
with the scary statistics
from my research

as she finishes my makeover.
She listens politely
and "mm-hmms" in the right places.
She doesn't ask any questions, though.
And when I mention that Massachusetts
is on the verge of passing a plastic bag ban
and maybe she could
call her local congressperson
to express support,
she says, simply,
"Good idea."

I wrap it up.

"Take a look," she says proudly,
steering me to my bureau mirror.
I flutter my eyelids a few times.
The eye shadow is surprisingly pretty.
My first thought:
Will petition signers
take me more seriously
if I wear it?

Lee pulls out
some cobalt blue mascara and says,
"Will you try this on me?"

JUST TWO PIANISTS SINGING INTO THE SEA

On Saturday morning,
we go to the beach,
just because it's the last day of November
and we can.

Lee falls in love with the shells
as I did,
as I knew she would.
She finds an unbroken conch
and cradles it like treasure.

She tells me Mrs. Krasnova
has encouraged her to visualize
during pieces.
She showed Lee
the cross section of a nautilus shell.
Lee is supposed to imagine
spiraling to the center
during a part of her Beethoven sonata
that gets quieter
and more intense.
She laughs and says
it only works sometimes.

I tell her about R. Josefowitz's ideas
about turning performance into a
pleasure.

We sit on the sand
and sing the goofy words
to Beethoven's Fifth Symphony
we made up in fifth grade.

"TU-NA ON *WHEAT.*
TU-NA ON *RYE.*
We've got to eat
'cause if we don't
we're gonna die,

"and for dessert
I really want
a piece of *pie* . . ."

Not Shakespeare, exactly,
but music
to my ears.

GRAND OPENING

Uncle Chris once said
that no one is ever bored
at a Greek wedding.

All the Trident Restaurant's grand opening is missing
is two people in love
with flower crowns on their heads.

My uncle got
a bouzouki band from Fort Myers
to play for cheap.
The string plucks
zoom around the room
and buzz in my ears
like mosquitoes.
At times, the melodies fly so fast,
I lose my own breath listening.

The air smells like roasted meat,
garlic, lemon juice,
and oregano.
People wave
their souvlaki skewers around
as they talk over the music.

Aegean blue and limestone white
feature in the tiling . . .
There are also bronze lights
and light wood chairs
and a funky stone bar.

I saw the renovations in stages.
Tonight, I'm glad
my dad got his way
and splurged on the design.
Lee keeps shouting about how
beautiful
everything looks.

My cousin Stephanie comes over
to hug both of us.
She met Lee once on a visit to Massachusetts.

We head to a table
and devour filo pastries
so soaked with honey
we have to lick our fingers.

It's my party . . .
I might have dessert for dinner!

THE FAMILY LASKARIS, RESTAURATEURS

My mother looks
as glamorous as Ms. Alvarez.
Her eyelashes practically touch her eyebrows.
She shakes every guest's hand,
explains what's in the food,
points me out
to strangers.
I wave across the room
to make a good impression.

My dad flits
in and out of the kitchen,
restocking the tables,
uncorking wine.

When things are humming,
he and Uncle Chris
throw out their arms
and do a zeibekiko dance
in front of the band.
The crowd cheers and whistles.

The restaurant business is tough.
I know this packed party

doesn't mean the Trident
will succeed.

If it fails,
it won't be from lack of effort.

ORDINARY FRIENDSHIPS

Lee and Stephanie meet the Lowells.
Henry's plate is piled high with food.
Anne is wearing all white clothing
with turquoise jewelry.

The Lowells want to hear about my petition
and confirm the date
for the beach cleanup next month.

"I told everyone at school about it.
I don't know if they'll come," I add,
but Henry and Anne say not to worry.

I'm surprised
when I see kids I know.
Harper and Grace and their families are here.
They saw the grand opening advertised
in the *Wilford Islander*.
When I introduce Lee and Stephanie,
it feels nice.
New friends meeting old friends.
Proof that I'm an ordinary, likable
human being.

No sign of Carmen, though.

But Ethan came
with his entire family!
"We love Greek food," his mom tells my mom.
Ethan greets me with "Hey, activist!"
and gives me a high five.
I ask him if he's heard
from the *Islander* yet,
but he says no.

Afterward, Lee's eyes are playful.
"Who was *that?*"

I shake my head.
"Just a friend."

That alone feels good to say.

AFTER-PARTY

Lee and I stay up so late,
until the final loud guests
stumble out
after a fifth baklava each
and zeibekiko dancing lessons
from my father.

My mom wants to drive us home,
but we're wired
and whine that we want to stay.

We all clean up together,
the way we used to
back home.
Lee grins,
loading plate after plate
into our rapid-wash dishwasher —
her favorite thing.

I see some pieces of cellophane
in the garbage,
but I pick them out
without making a fuss.
My parents have always
recycled their aluminum food trays

and used
compostable to-go containers
at their restaurants.

I don't want to disturb the way
they're looking at each other right now —
triumphantly,
as if they each performed
the best piano piece of their life
onstage at Carnegie Hall.

EVENING FLIGHT

We all sleep late,
and I wake up sad.
Today is the day Lee is leaving.

We make chocolate chip pancakes
for lunch
and leave the counter a sticky mess.

We spend a little time
pulling limp leaves
off my garden plants
and watching videos
on my laptop.

When my mom asks her
to play one of her
competition pieces,
I expect Lee to refuse.
Instead, she says,
"Sure. I should practice, anyway."

She springs off the couch
to the piano,
limbers up with a couple of scales,

and plays.

PRECISE LANGUAGE

In a recent homeroom exercise
aimed at giving us "tools" to express our feelings,
I learned the difference
between jealousy and envy.

Jealousy is being afraid
of getting hurt
or losing something you have.

Envy is longing for
something you don't have
and feeling resentful toward the person
who has it.

I guess I couldn't hear it before
through the phone.
Lee doesn't play Bach's Fantasia in C Minor
like someone a year better
than she was last year.

She plays like a concert pianist.
As if she's done nothing but practice
since I left for Florida.
As if she's quit regular school
and started studying at Curtis or Eastman

or some other dream conservatory.
Which I know she hasn't . . .
so how is she so good?

I'm envious.

UNPREPARED

I applaud and hoot loudly
to conceal my envy.

"Now you, Mimi!" Lee says.
My father and mother
add their encouragement.

I cannot play a note in front of anyone
right now.

I close my eyes
and shake my head,
and the other three people in my house
think I'm just being modest,
don't realize I'm about to cry.
They make sounds of dismay
when I storm into my bedroom.

I press tissues to my eyes
to keep in the tears.

LIFE REWIND

"Mimi?"
Lee knocks softly and enters.

"You were incredible, really —" I begin.
She waves away the compliment.

"So are you.
You don't have to play now.
We're both tired.
But — do you want to talk?"

My words tumble out
in an uneven tempo.
"I haven't been practicing enough,
and my grades are slipping a tiny bit
because I'm really focused on canvassing.
It's because I have less time,
but it's also because" —
I admit to Lee and to myself —
"some days,
practicing doesn't feel as important.
But then I hear you,
and I want to be that good
because I do love piano . . ."

Lee nods.
"What you're doing for the environment
is amazing.
But maybe —
it could be more like a hobby?
Or an extracurricular?
You're so talented.
You have an actual shot at conservatory study.
There aren't many people who can say that!
I don't think you should throw it away,
you know?"
She makes her pouty frown face
and then wraps me in a hug.

I know.
I know that's what she thinks,
and what my parents must think,
and what I'm supposed to think.

I have a dark thought
as we all pile into the car
to drive Lee to the airport:

If we'd never moved here,
I might never have watched Melati and Isabel's video
and never thought hard about single-use plastic waste,
and I'd still be Mrs. Krasnova's student

back home,
practicing as hard as Lee,

and life would be simpler.

CONTROL

For the next week
I come straight home from school
and practice.

I get a little better,
and I enjoy taking the time
to go over the tricky parts,
to play chords and slowly break them
into arpeggios,
to consider the exact mood
of the sections.
I play with purpose.

I keep the petition
zippered
in my backpack,
so I don't have to look at it.

THE BOY WHO LIKES JOURNALISM

Maybe Carmen has worked magic.

I check the online petition.
The signatures are up to
eighty-four.
Better,
but not good enough.

I need to get back to canvassing.

I roll an idea around
like a pearl.

Maybe,
I'm not sure,
but is it crazy to think
that Ethan
might want to help me?

He could bring his microphone to Frank's
and interview islanders
who sign the petition —
and islanders who don't.
Gather data,
like Ms. Miller suggests,

and get a *Scaled Fish* episode
out of it.

A team of two
instead of
one.

REJECTION

Part of me hopes
I'll run into Ethan outside Frank's
and share my idea . . .
but that never happens.

Before I summon the nerve
to write him,
he emails me.

NO LUCK WITH THE ISLANDER
is his message.

He has forwarded their response:

YOUR CAUSE IS NOTEWORTHY
BUT THE ISLANDER MAINTAINS HIGH STANDARDS
OF JOURNALISTIC INTEGRITY
AND PUBLISHES OPINION PIECES THAT ARE BOTH
THOUGHT-PROVOKING AND
WELL WRITTEN.
FROM YOUR LETTER'S
LACK OF CARE AND FLUENCY,
WE ARE AFRAID WE MUST DECLINE
YOUR REQUEST.

"I THOUGHT THIS WOULD MAKE A INTERESTING EDIROTRIAL AND I HOPE YOUD AGREE"

Ethan's original letter,
which follows the rejection,
is an inarticulate pile
of seagull droppings.

I CAN'T HELP MYSELF

I'M NOT SURPRISED THEY SAID NO.

YOU SHOULD HAVE ASKED ME TO WRITE THE EMAIL.

OR AT LEAST TO PROOFREAD YOURS!

I hit SEND before
the cloud of red
in my vision
makes me add something meaner.

AVOIDANCE

Ethan doesn't respond.

It doesn't feel good to put
distance between myself and someone else
at such a small school,

but I swivel my head
in the opposite direction
if we pass each other
in the hall.

It's not the end of the world.
The *Wilford Islander*
might still pick up the story
if we get five hundred signatures.
I collected a few dozen
outside Frank's

and the beach cleanup
is approaching.
One hundred and twenty or so more
and we're there.
Anne and Henry say that
they're working extra hard to get people
to come this year.

Ms. Miller offered
to remind all her classes
about it.

I'm thinking we'll need
a table with a cloth and our posters,
so I find Carmen
and ask if she's planning
to bring them.

"Yeah, sure," she says
before
(am I seeing things?)
swiveling her head
in the opposite direction.

SAD GARDEN

I pace in the backyard
and FaceTime Lee after school
to remind myself
that I still have one friend.
(Well, there's Stephanie,
but she's related.)

We talk delicately
about piano and plastic bags.
I mostly turn the camera
so she can see the tomato leaves
that look like puzzle pieces
and the weird white, squiggly lines
on the spinach.

I douse the stalks with hose water
to spray away pests —
another thing I should be doing every day
but don't.

Henry gave us a sample
of his homemade insecticide soap
when I described the problems.
I give the plants a few targeted
squirts.

"I don't remember our plants back home
ever looking this bad," I say.
I haven't asked my dad for help,
since he comes home after I go to bed
seven days a week.
Every night,
he leaves a little pile of clothes
that smell like grill grease
in the laundry room.

"It snowed half an inch here, today.
Growing tomatoes in December at all
is some kind of miracle!"
Lee replies
before signing off to go practice.

NINE P.M. TEXT

It's from Carmen:

CHECK TWITTER COMMENTS

ORGANIZED ATTACK

I thought I'd find more
creepy reactions
to Carmen's selfies.

Instead,
trolls have crept out
from under their bridges
and rocks
and spewed ignorance
in comments that go
on and on.

Some argue that climate change
is a hoax.

More unload that they are
fed up with youth movements,
with the self-righteous Gretas
and Melatis and Isabels
of the world —
frauds,
whom the media brainwash
and then fawn over.

One has edited the photo
of Carmen dangling the plastic bag
on the stick.
Printed across its crinkled surface
are the words BAG OF LIES.

One talks about hurting Carmen —
and that's when I stop reading
and call her.

RIP @WIPLASTICBAGBOYCOTT

I wonder when Carmen stopped reading.
The serene vegetarian dolphin lover
speaks in a crushed-glass voice
that cracks and chips.

"I can't believe
they would say those things.
They don't even
know me.
Do you think
they know me?"

"Probably not" is my reply
because I can't say
no
with certainty.
"Lots of young activists get trolled."
I remember reading about this ugliness.
"Girls and nonwhite kids
are targeted most often," I tell Carmen.
"The attacks are disturbing,
but they're probably not personal."

"They definitely *feel* personal."

"Yeah, but —"

"You don't know what it was like" —
her voice rises —
"to check my posts,
like no big deal,
and read those things about me."

I don't answer.
A little part of me imagines that
maybe they wouldn't have come after the account
if I'd curated it
with my boring bulleted lists.
But maybe they would have.
Cruelty isn't rational.

I hear Ms. Alvarez's
urgent-sounding voice in the background.

"My parents want me to shut down
all the accounts," says Carmen.

"Oh . . .
but if you do,
how are we going to get —"

"I'm shutting them down," says Carmen.

"I'll talk to you later."

WHAT REALLY MATTERS

I go to bed troubled
that our movement has no more social media.

I wake up worrying about Carmen.

I arrive early to school
and stop her on the path
before the Charybdis of her admirers
whirls near.
"I'm so sorry you went through that," I say.
"Those attacks were disgusting.
How are you doing?"

Today, her hair hangs straight.
No goddess waves.
She tucks some strands behind her ear.
"Fine."

"Are you sure?
I wouldn't be fine."

A tiny pinch of a frown
creases her brow.
"Thanks for your concern."

I tell myself
that I'm imagining the sarcasm.

"So, the beach cleanup
is in a week,
and you might not want to do anything,
and that's completely okay.
But I'm going to try to knock on some doors
because the only way —"

"Stop, Mimi. Just stop.
There are three reasons
I'm not going to help you anymore."

I know what's coming
is going to hurt
like walking on broken shells.

WHY CARMEN ISN'T SAYING NO TO PLASTIC BAGS ON WILFORD ISLAND

"The first reason is,
all I have in my head are those comments,
and I need a break to get over them."

This, I understand perfectly.

"Second, my dad is making me.
He doesn't really believe reusable bags
will catch on here,
and he doesn't want
to charge his customers for paper bags.
They're more expensive than you think
in the long run.
He runs a customer-first business."

I imagine Mr. Hill
putting a slick gloss on those lines
for his daughter
while extending a palmful of pomegranate seeds.
Sometimes deceitful deities
live in sunlit places.

"The third reason is because
I'm not sure you like me very much."

Urchin spines spear my foot.

"Excuse me?"

FIGHT SCENE

CARMEN
Why didn't you invite me to
your restaurant opening?
I heard how much of a party it was
at school on Monday.

MIMI
I didn't invite anybody! They just came!

CARMEN
Well, that's weird, don't you think?
Friends invite friends to things.

MIMI
Yeah, well,
friends also ask friends
to eat lunch with them.

CARMEN
Are you kidding?
I came over to sit at your lunch table,
and you didn't ask me to stay!

MIMI
You didn't want to stay!

CARMEN

I did. But you were clearly happy
with your other friends.

MIMI
(exploding)
I have no friends here! NONE!

CARMEN
(beat)
You have to be a friend
to make a friend.
Try it sometime.
(Carmen exits.)

END SCENE

HEAD SWIVELS

It is difficult
to avoid two people
at one tiny school.

REGRESSION

When Kyle asks
why the rainstorm in my Chopin nocturne
sounds like globs of mud
falling from the sky
and the Liszt has more
sloppy mistakes
in it than last week,
I start to cry.

The tears don't pool
this time —
they drip down my cheeks,
through the cracks between my fingers.

I can't play another note
in this little practice room
with the orchid on the stand in the corner
next to Kyle's rolled-up yoga mat.

My mother insists
that I blow my nose
and finish the lesson,

but Kyle suggests we break.

My mother whispers something,
and Kyle answers,

"We'll see."

GODDESS WALK

That night,
it's nine ... ten ... eleven p.m. ...
Sleep doesn't come.

I poke my fingers
between my window blinds
and peer at the backyard,

at the full moon illuminating
my vanquished
vegetable garden.

I listen for noise from my parents' room
and sneak out the back door.

The night air is
heavy with moisture
and smells like salt.

It's not fair.
Tropical flowers flourish on this island,
but nothing I grow
survives.

I pull one sickly plant out
of the ground.
Another.
I use both hands
to unstake them,
to hurl them into the air.
Flying,
they are comets of soil
and bug-chewed leaves.

Soon, a bed of disturbed earth
is all that's left.

I tremble at my
dirty fingertips and
raw destruction.

MORTALITY RESTORED

Before I go inside,
I pile the unearthed plants neatly
so that my night harvest doesn't look
like complete

madness.

AVOIDANCE II

My parents settle me on the couch
for a talk the following morning.

"So many tears," my mother says,
caressing the back of my head.
"Tell us what's going on,
Demetra."

I give them a line about
school, piano, and the plastic bag movement
being a lot.

"You know,
you can take as much time as you need
to get those signatures," she says.
"Take the year. There's no rush."

No rush . . .
except for the millions of plastic bags
Wilford Islanders could avoid throwing away *this* year
if I filled the petition
and brought it before the town council
in January.

"What if you skipped
the beach cleanup?" my father asked.

I close that idea down quickly.
"It's just one Saturday afternoon.
The Lowells are planning it anyway,
not me."

The beach cleanup
is helping me
keep it together
because it's something
I can think about
so I don't have to think about everything else.

"I can do it all.
I just need to organize my time
better."

"Are you sure there's nothing else
bothering you, loulouthi mou?"
my father asks.
He was out on the deck
with his morning coffee,
so I know he saw the garden
and the empty plant graves.

But he didn't say anything
when he came in.

I wish we'd never come here.
I want to go home.
These complaints
do no good
because my parents have worked so hard
on the restaurant,
and it seems to be doing okay
so we're staying.

I shake my head and smile.

My mom slaps her legs.
"Then seize the day!" she says,
and points at the piano.

I HAVE TO QUIT PIANO OR PLASTICS

I practice
emptily.

Scales aren't fun anymore
when they don't help my fingers
handle Liszt's runs.

I'm tired of one section
flowing like water
and another splattering
messes of notes everywhere.

I'm afraid of my pieces.

MY PROBLEMS TURN SMALL

Anne calls from the hospital
midweek
to tell us that Henry was moving a garden bench
when he had

a heart attack.

FOURTH MOVEMENT

SLOW-MOTION PHONE CALL

My mind refuses
to conjure a picture of
that tall, deep-voiced man
crumpling.

He has to rest and be monitored
at a hospital in Fort Myers.

The Lowells are canceling
the beach cleanup.

"Just for the time being,"
Anne tells me,
"but let your school friends know, Mimi."

"What do you need?"
my mom asks Anne
when she gets the phone back.
"Should we check on the bookstore?"

My mother listens carefully
to Anne's answer,
then hangs up.
"We're going to Fort Myers.

We'll stop by the restaurant first
to bring them a little something."

"Did Anne say it was okay?"

My mom kisses me on the cheek.
"She said seeing you
would cheer Henry up."

RECOVERY

The part of the hospital we're in
smells like old people.
I read the names written in marker
outside the patients' doors,
wanting to see Henry's
and nervous to see Henry's.

To my surprise,
he's sitting in a chair,
not the bed,
sipping coffee from a white cup.
He looks okay —
his face is just a little grayer than usual.

I've never seen Anne dressed so plainly.
She's wearing a beige T-shirt
and khaki capris.

"Joni," Henry says
in a mellow voice.
"I'm so sorry to have let you down.
I'll be back on my feet in no time."

I tell him not to worry about it,
please.
I ask what happened.

"Eh, it was coming for me," Henry says.
"Runs in the family.
My father had heart disease —

"but I can stand to eat more veggies
and play more tennis, too,"
he adds when Anne raises her eyebrows.

My mom presents the bagged-up entrées
we brought for Anne
so she wouldn't have to cook at home.
Anne jokes that
she will finally get to finish
an entire piece of pastitsio
without Henry nibbling off her plate.

We talk about the hospital stay
and the excellent nurses
until Henry says,

"Tell us where you are with the movement.
How's the petition?"

And I wonder if it's intentional
that my mother chooses that moment
to make a phone call outside.

Anne moves to the bed's edge
and gives me her chair.

"I'm,
well . . .
I'm a little stuck," I begin.

WOULD I DARE?

I tell Anne and Henry
that Frank's won't stock different bags,
that I lost a shot at an editorial in the *Islander*
and have no more social media
and may have driven away the two other kids
who were willing to help me.
I tell them
that I can't see how I'll be effective
going to the town council
alone
with fewer than four hundred signatures.

"Will you still do it?" Anne asks.

It's not what I'm expecting her to say.
"Should I?"

"We can't decide that for you."
Anne clasps her hands in her lap.
"The question is
whether you're committed enough
to this cause
to keep moving forward."

"I am. But —
I don't think anything's
going to change."

"The first time I wanted to run for selectperson
in Connecticut," says Anne,
"I didn't get enough signatures to get on the ballot.
Then I did. And I lost."

Henry chuckles. "That was a tough night."

Anne's face stays serious.
"Well, sure it was,
but I knew my ideas were good ones,
so I ran again.
And won.
And made the schools and the library
and the recycling program
in our little town
better.
With activism,
there are always setbacks.
Even those capable sisters on Bali
you told us about
had setbacks, I'm sure."

"Anne's right."
Henry's eyes flash.
"Here's an idea, Joni —
why don't you reach out
to those girls for advice?
Even thunderclaps like you and Anne
need support sometimes."

He pats his wife's knee.
"I know I do."

PARKING LOT PARTY

When the nurse tells us we have to leave,
my mother and I give Henry
gentle hugs
and remind Anne to call
if she needs anything.

When we get to the parking lot,
my dad's pulling in —
too late for visiting hours.

No matter.
We call Henry's room
and tell him to look out the window,
and we wave and blow kisses
and jump up and down
on the pavement.

I was wrong about having
no friends on Wilford Island.
The two I have
just happen to be in their
seventies.

SIGNIFICANT LETTER

On the drive home,
I go from thinking there's no way
I could ever bother Melati and Isabel —
who have spoken to the United Nations,
for goodness' sake —

to staring at their photo on my phone
and remembering that
one of their goals
is to empower young people everywhere . . .

to composing half my letter to them
in my head.

When I get home,
instead of practicing
or studying for my social studies test,
questions
pour from my fingertips
onto my laptop keyboard.
I proofread the letter —
then shut my eyes

and decide not to hit SEND.

LESSON NUMBER ONE

Something strange happens
when I write the letter.
I see answers
in my questions.

If they were to respond,
I already know what Melati and Isabel
would say.

I know I've had good ideas
and worked hard,
but I've also been a little bit
stupid.

And afraid.

Lesson number one, Melati said.
You cannot do it all by yourself.

It was right there,
that day in Ms. Miller's class.

I write a new letter
in which I thank them for their work
and for inspiring

me and kids like me
all over the world

and send that instead.

REPAIR WORK BEGINS

On Saturday morning
I ride to Ethan Hoffman's house
with two reusable bags.

"Hi," I say
when he comes to the door
with doubtful eyes.

My apology for my reaction
to Ethan's editorial rejection
isn't perfect —
I stammer some —
but it does contain the words
obnoxious and
unfair.

"Today would have been
the wildlife refuge beach cleanup."
I hold out the bags.
"I was wondering —
do you want to come with me
and pick up trash anyway?
I could use the help."

ETHAN'S TRUTH

The December breezes
off the sea
make the drawstrings of our hoodies
dance.

As we put potato chip wrappers
and bottle caps into our bags,

Ethan talks about his
learning disability in written expression
that wasn't properly diagnosed
until a few years ago.

All the good feelings
from my apology
sink into shame.

He seems to read my face.
"Don't feel bad for me.
I'm as smart as anyone.
My brain just works differently
when I write.

"And I'm sorry, too," he continues.
"My learning specialist keeps reminding me

to think about
audience.
An essay for school
needs more revision
than a text to a friend.
I know this.
I was just so excited
about the editorial request
that I rushed it."

"I get it," I say.
"Hey —
is that why
you do podcasts?
With spoken interviews?"

I feel like a genius for making this
obvious connection.

"It's part of it," he says.
"It's bigger than that.
I'm like you.
I want to make change
by telling the truth about things."

He looks a little embarrassed
after he says this

and picks up a pair of sandy take-out cups
in silence,

but I like him more than ever.

REPAIR WORK CONTINUES

I ride to Carmen's house
on Sunday.

I'm worried she might be in Miami —
or Maui —
but she comes to the door
when I text that I'm outside.

Her hair is up in a topknot
so I can't tell
if she's back to curling it yet.

I ask how she's doing,
if she still thinks about the Twitter comments,
if she feels safe.

She shrugs. "It's better. A little."

I say that I'm sorry,
and I've thought a lot
about what she said,
and I should have invited her
to the Trident Restaurant's grand opening.

Because I want to be her friend,

even though she has
a million friends already.

"It just looks that way," she says.
"I'm closer to my sister
than to anyone at Wilford School.
We never fight."

I wonder if Liliana
is the reason Carmen looks and acts
older than the rest of us.
"I'm glad you got to visit her
in Miami that time," I say.

A current of pain
flashes across her face.
"Yeah. Once."

I stay quiet
and leave space
for other words to come out.

"I thought she'd come home more,
you know?
And give me books she'd read
like she used to
and drive us to beaches.

But she barely texts.
When I see her,
her face is different —
it sort of glows
when she talks about her classes
and the people she's meeting."

Carmen wraps her arms
around her body.

"I get it. I mean, college is a big deal.
But she's there and I'm here.
So, when you joined our class . . .
well, I'm glad you did."

It's tricky
to be the girl
who leaves all she knows for a new place.
What I never thought about
is that sometimes it's just as tricky
to be the girl
left behind.

STALEMATE

I thank Carmen for telling me all this.

"Come eat with me anytime at school," she says.
"I should have made that clear."

It's an opening.
I glance reflexively behind her,
at her home-makeover after-shot
of an entryway.
"You might get angry at me
all over again . . .
but could we meet with your dad
and ask him —
flat out —
to pay
for alternative grocery bags at Frank's?"

She chews her lip as she looks at me.
"I love it when you go full earth goddess."

"*Stop saying that.*
You're the one people listen to."

A sad smile. "If that were true,
we'd have a full petition."

Carmen steps off the threshold
and speaks under her breath.
"I did argue with my dad.
Even my mom did,
but we can't convince him,
so I don't know what to do."

MODERN GODDESSES AREN'T STATUES

I tell her what I saw
between the lines
of my letter to Melati and Isabel.
My vision.
Ethan high-fived me
when he heard it.
"If anything will wake up this sleepy island,
that will!" he said.

"If Frank Hill's daughter is involved,"
I say to Carmen,
"that would apply
a special kind of pressure,
don't you think?"

Carmen blows air out
through her mouth.
"He's my dad.
I have to think about it."

"We're *both* earth goddesses."
It feels silly and bold,
at the same time,
to say it,
but Carmen drifted back

to me for a reason.
Reunited,
we can revive the planet.
"Let's do more than love
dolphins and fish,
birds and humans.
Let's save them."

No smile returned this time,
Carmen's face is all heavy,
no light.
"I'll text you," she says,
and glides into her house.

OBSESSION CONFESSION

On Monday, I interrupt
nervous chatter around the lunch table
about the math quiz
to say that I have something
important to talk about.

I take out the lists of middle schoolers
I printed last night
and describe my plan
to Harper, Caroline, Grace, Zoe, and Skylar.

Harper's mouth opens a little.

Before,
that expression
would have twisted and tangled my convictions
like seaweed around a lure.
Not now.
I'm done being super chill
when so much is at stake.

"You've all been so nice to me.
I'm nervous about asking for help
because I don't want you to think
I'm the weird girl from Massachusetts

who thinks only about plastic bags . . .
but I kind of am!"

Zoe laughs.

"So, should we do this?"

"Yes," Grace says
without hesitation —
as I'd hoped,
though her support still warms me
like sunbaked sand.
"It'll be powerful, Mimi."
She grabs the sheet that lists the seventh-graders
and starts writing her initials
by some of the names.

Caroline's sister is in sixth grade.
She agrees
to take a chunk of kids from that list.

"Harper and I could talk to
the eighth-grade tennis players,"
says Skylar. "Right?"

Harper looks around the table,
and the pause,

which I'm expecting to be
dramatic,
is, in fact,
barely noticeable.

"Yeah."
She reaches for a sheet.
"I'm in. Cool idea, Mimi."

Maybe I convinced her.
Or maybe
it's that everyone wants to
fit in.
Or maybe
she was always

my friend.

HEART REPAIR

I stop by the Dusty Jacket
to see Anne
and hear about Henry.
I help her unpack and sort
book cartons
in the upstairs room.

I'm happy to see
she's wearing
a purple denim jacket
with a splatter-paint print.

"Oh, he's grumping about,"
she says of Henry,
"singing ballads to bacon and waffles
and everything else
he can't eat anymore.
He takes a walk to the store
once a day
and walks home again
and then has a nap.
He's itching to come back
to work.
Soon enough."

Her eyes get misty
and she looks straight at me.
"We got lucky that time,
didn't we, Mimi?"

I nod and give her
the tightest hug I can.

THE BEST TEACHER ON EARTH

We can put my plan in place
with the teachers' help —
or keep everything secret
so they don't try to stop us.

I know what Melati and Isabel
would do,
especially if Ms. Miller
were their teacher.

"Oh, my," she says
when I ask for a meeting in study hall
the day before
our plan goes into effect.
She thinks for a long time.
"It needs to be safe."

I nod.
"It should be.
Parents will know.
Kids can bring
water, medicine —
anything they might need."

"I have to tell Ms. Cameron
and Mr. LeRoux."

Our principal and vice principal —
who were so
friendly and funny
when they showed me around
Wilford School last August
and then morphed into
authority figures
in September,
surveying us all
with smiles that said,
*We believe in you and
don't disappoint us.*

I figured Ms. Miller would
tell them.

"Please say we're sorry
for the disruption,
but pollution and climate change are real,
backed up by science,
and we're doing something about it."

Ms. Miller crosses her arms
and smiles, as if I'm the farthest thing

from a disappointment.
I feel seen
by my teacher,
who is crazy obsessed
with unusual and awesome things, too.

"Okay.
What else do you need from me?"

"Just one thing.
Could you call the *Wilford Islander*
and let them know?
I want to be sure
reporters take us
seriously."

PREPARATIONS

That night,
I pedal around
to the houses on my list,
dropping off repurposed cardboard
for posters,
paint,
and fat markers
in azure blue,
emerald green,
rebellious red —
all colors
Anne would approve of.

I text with my lunch table friends,
who are doing the same.
We raided our homes
for supplies
and, with Ms. Miller's help,
borrowed the rest
from the storage closet at school.
It's fun to read
their giddy words
and see their selfies
on the thread.

Ethan's ready, too.
Even though
our texts flutter back and forth,
his words are thoughtful
and mostly spelled correctly.
Not that I care.

At eight p.m.
Carmen texts me.
I'M IN,
AND I HAVE A SURPRISE FOR YOU.
MAYBE.
I HOPE IT WORKS OUT.
#EARTHGODDESSES

My reply:
I'M SO GLAD.
I CAN'T WAIT.
JUST YOU BEING THERE IS ENOUGH.
#EARTHGODDESSES

FORGIVENESS, NOT PERMISSION

I stay quiet in my room
until after ten p.m.
when I hear my father come home.

It's cowardly
to wait so long,
but I want my parents together.
Dad buffers Mom's
storm tide displeasure
like a bulwark.
Sometimes.

"Mimi, you should be asleep!"
says my mother.
"And did you practice today?"

I take it as an opening.
"No. I couldn't.
I've been planning something . . ."

They listen.
And look at each other.

"I love it," says my father,
clapping his hands

and rubbing them together.
"You're our daughter, all right.
That's the Laskaris passion,
right there."

The Laskaris passion
does not concern my mother
the way my future does.
"Demetra,"
she says slowly,
"are you going to get expelled
from the only school
on this island?"

"*Probably* not,"
I reply.
"But I am going
to change
this island.
I hope."

WALKOUT

At ten a.m.
on Thursday, December 12th,
one hundred one middle schoolers
at Wilford School
pushed out their desk chairs
and walked out of class.

They fetched their homemade posters
in the halls,
and though they'd been instructed to be
silent and respectful,
they chattered with anticipation.

They were all wearing sneakers —
not flip-flops
or platform sandals.

Many of them hooked water bottles
into their belt straps.
Some put on caps
and sunglasses.

Ms. Miller held the front door
of the school open
and looked each student

in the eye
with concern
and pride
as they exited.

The other middle school teachers
flanked them
as they spilled onto Main Street.

Four middle schoolers
stayed behind,
unmoved by the "garbage march,"
as one eighth-grader called it.

Their choice.

When the giant crowd
had left the building,
signs
and voices

were lifted.

YOU WERE RIGHT, MELATI

Until ten o'clock came,
and the hallways filled
with keyed-up kids,

each of whom
had been contacted personally by
Harper, Caroline, Grace, Zoe, Skylar, Ethan, or me,

I still thought
I might be the only one
walking out of Wilford School
on this impossibly warm and breezy
December day.

Look around.
I am not doing it all
by myself.

MAIN STREET SYNCOPATIONS

I'm a pianist.
My singing voice sounds
a lot like a hoarse goat,
I've always thought.

But that doesn't stop me
from leading the first chant
from the front of the line.

"Hey, hey!
Ho, ho!
Plastic bags have got to go!"

Instantly
we're marching to the beat
and making our signs dance,
and Ethan next to me
is working
some groovy shoulder action —

the kid has moves!

PROTEST SIGNS

The signs around me
are varied and clever,
with large blue letters, green earths,
and red lines through plastic bags.

We sent around some ideas . . .

> SAY NO TO PLASTIC BAGS ON WILFORD ISLAND
>
> PLASTICS KILL SEA LIFE
>
> KEEP OUR ISLAND BEAUTIFUL
>
> REDUCE REUSE RECYCLE

. . . but some kids got personal:

> STOP PASSING OUT PLASTIC & LET ME GET BACK TO
> CLASS!
>
> HOLY MACKEREL! FISH SURE TASTE BETTER WITHOUT
> MICROPLASTICS
>
> HEY TOWN COUNCIL, IT'S MY FUTURE ON THE LINE

Mine says simply

> WILFORD ISLAND IS NOT DISPOSABLE

SOMETHING MISSING

Harper, of all people,
wants to lead a chant.
We have a hurried conference,
and she and Grace
model a call-and-response:

"What do we want?"
"A plastic boycott!"
"When do we want it?"
"*Now!*"

The kids catch on.
Harper keeps going.

I see a lot of seventh-graders
around me,
but one is missing.

I maneuver my way
through the marchers,
find Carmen,
hair curled,
thick-soled sneakers
completely on trend.
I pull her to the front.

This time, I'm the Gulf wind,
and she looks surprised
to be blown out of hiding.

"This is *our* movement!"
I shout at her.
"I can't change the world without you."

Carmen smiles.
Her sign says
I SPEAK FOR THE DOLPHINS:
NO MORE PLASTIC BAGS IN OUR OCEANS

She lifts it above her head
and yells,
"*Now!*"

FIFTY-MINUTE MARCH

It is 2.2 miles
from Wilford School
to the Dusty Jacket.

Orange traffic cones
block off intersections.
A police officer
reroutes cars
once we get to a busier part
of Main Street.

As a precaution
Ms. Miller notified the police
along with the press.

She
and a few other teachers
walk the whole way with us,
but on sidewalks.
The students are the only ones
in the streets.

We don't chant the whole time.
Sometimes a chant
dies away into embarrassed laughter

and we just talk
and walk.

But when people start peering out of stores
and I spy the plaza up ahead,
I blast a new chant
into the lazy Wilford Island morning:

"Our island!"
"Our future!"

"Our water!"
"Our future!"

"Our land!"
"Our future!"

"Our planet!"
"Our future!"

ANTHEM

In the Dusty Jacket plaza
stands one of Ethan's microphones
hooked up
to his older brother's amp.

As we approach,
Joni Mitchell's soulful voice
blasts from the open windows
of the Dusty Jacket.

She sings about apples, birds, and bees,
and taking care of what you have
while you still have it.

From the doorway, Anne —
and Henry! —
start clapping,

and then a hurricane of cheering
drowns out the music.
A shockingly large whorl
of islanders has gathered in the plaza:
the parents who took off work
to see the march;
the forceful army

of wildlife refuge volunteers;
the curious bystanders;
the teachers;
us.

The crowd raises cell phones
to take our pictures,
and we raise our signs higher.

MEDIA PRESENCE

As we shuffle into position,
I notice one
heavy-looking black video camera
on a man's shoulder up front —
then a second.
(*Two?*)
There are two news vans
parked on the curb as well.

One van says WILFORD ISLANDER.
The other says
FORT MYERS NEWS-PRESS.

"Reporters from Fort Myers are here!"
I buzz into Carmen's ear.

"Surprise . . ." she says.

COMEBACK KID

Ms. Alvarez
called the *News-Press*
and told them that her daughter suffered
online harassment
but emerged even more resolute
to save her beloved marine animals —
and if they didn't want to miss
the news story of the winter,
they'd better dart over the causeway.
Then Carmen grabbed the phone
and explained all about
the Wilford Island
student walkout.

Carmen whispers all this
to me quickly,
then flutters her fingers
at her beaming mother,
who is standing with
my parents!

My dad beams, too.
My mother . . .
I wouldn't call it beaming,
but her eyes are big

as she takes in the crowd,
the kids,
the signs,
the reporters.

Impressed, maybe?

I AM A VESSEL

It's time.
I step forward
and the crowd quiets.

Something comes over me —
nerves, I guess,
but instead of running me aground,
they make me feel
as if I've caught a breeze,
as if everything has already been set
into motion
and I must simply sail to Ethan's microphone
and say what's in my heart
because my message is not about me,
it's about the earth
and the truth.

REBELS WITH A CAUSE

When they met with Bali's governor,
Melati and Isabel
were clear and direct.

I lay out our demands:

One. We'd like all Wilford Island businesses
to stop distributing plastic bags.

Two. We'd like the town council
to consider our petition,
signed by three hundred eighty-nine residents.
We'd like them to vote
on a resolution
to reduce plastic waste
and to support businesses
in providing alternative bags.

Three. We'd like all residents to pledge
to bring their own bags
when they shop.

"We're kids
who should be in school,
doing math

and reading poetry,
not worrying about
toxins
and dead sea life
and garbage patches
and the fate of the earth.
Help us, please.
This is our home," I say,

and for the first time,
home
is exactly how I think
of this precious island
I'm standing on.

AMBUSH

Carmen takes the mike next.

"Thanks for coming.
My father is Frank Hill,
the owner of Frank's,
and I'm going to ask him a question."

As she presses her cell phone screen,
I see her fingers
shake.

"Go, Carmen," I say
under my breath.

Mr. Hill's face appears
on the screen.
"Carmen? Are you all right?"

Carmen's throat ripples
as she swallows.
"I'm great, Dad."
She lifts the phone
so it slowly scans the kids,
then the crowd.
"I'm in the bookstore plaza

with my classmates
and some citizens
and some reporters.
We marched out of classes
this morning
for the environment,
and we want to know
if Frank's will stop
using plastic bags.

"Everyone can hear you, by the way."

CHANGE

The faintest "Uh . . ."

and then —
I have never heard Frank Hill
sound so generous.

"Frank's has always
been there for Wilford Islanders.
Part of that commitment
is caring for the island itself.
Carmen, honey, you have my word,"
his talking head says
into the microphone.
The breeze blows his words around
like salt spray.
"No more plastic bags.
We'll stock paper bags,
and shoppers are welcome
to purchase reusable Frank's bags
for $2.99."

No more
ghosts
will float into the world
from Frank's.

I'm the first to whoop,
and soon all the kids
are banging on posters
while the crowd applauds.
Carmen looks at me
as if she can't believe
what just happened.

I give her a huge hug
and whisper,

"Goddess, you're fearless!"

SIGNIFICANT OBSERVER

Reporters approach Carmen and me
and ask about our movement.
I catch Ethan staring at us
and pull him over for the interviews.
We tell our story.
When I get steaming mad about single-use plastics,
Ethan backs me up
and Carmen brings the light and hope
that things are about to change.

We hug our friends.
Kids I don't know well
tell me this was super fun
and if I have any other causes,
they'll walk out of school with me
anytime.

Some get rides back to school
with their parents.
Most walk
because it will take longer.

I'm talking to my parents,
who whisper
that they're exploding with pride

yet smile modestly
every time a new person comes up
to thank me for caring about Wilford Island.

Anne leads someone over to us,
a mostly bald man
in a white, short-sleeve dress shirt.

"Mimi? This is
Councilmember Richard Vaughan."

I wait for her to go on,
but then I get it.
Councilmember.

"It's nice to meet you, sir," I say.
"I represent Say No to Plastic Bags on Wilford Island.
I hope we can bring our petition
to your next town council meeting.
I really don't want to miss
any more school
marching for this cause."

ITEM 7.A.

Despite having fewer
than five hundred petition signatures,
we're on the agenda
for the January
Wilford Island Town Council meeting!

Between now and then
I have a lot to do.

I ADMIRE GRETA, BUT I'M STAYING ENROLLED FOR NOW

First on my list
is not to fail seventh grade.

It feels good to dive into
my schoolwork
and do decently on every teacher's
final test
before winter break.

Decently, not perfectly.

I mislabeled constitutional amendments
in social studies,
made careless ratio mistakes
on my math quiz,
and messed up amino acids sequencing
for Ms. Miller,
who wrote

"Oops! Guess you had other things
on your mind this month!"

in the margin.

I guess I did.

IT WOULD HAVE GONE DOWN DIFFERENTLY AT MY HOUSE

The second thing is
to be there for Carmen,
who had to face Frank Hill
after the walkout.

I call her that night.

When he got home from work,
Carmen told me that her mother fluttered around
and kissed her dad
and said what a wonderful man he was,
and how the dolphins were going to
live a little longer
because of his generosity.

Mr. Hill kissed his wife and daughter
and sat on the deck
with a quarter of a key lime pie
their housekeeper had made
and watched the sunset alone.

I don't quite understand
the Alvarez-Hill family,
but Ms. Alvarez is an earth goddess

like her daughter,
and at least Carmen didn't get into trouble.

FRIENDS AT WORK

I manage to avoid Mr. Hill
when I hang out with Carmen after school
the following week.
It's too windy to paddleboard,
so we just read our interviews aloud
and look at our photos
in the *Islander* and the *News-Press*
and giggle because we're kind of
famous!

Carmen's sister, Liliana,
texts a stream of words:
I CAN'T BELIEVE YOU DID THAT TO DAD.
CARMEN TERESA ALVAREZ-HILL,
YOU'RE SUCH A REBEL!
I'M PROUD OF YOU.
HOLD UP, SIS . . .
LOOK AT THIS!
THERE'S MENTION OF YOUR MARCH
IN THE MIAMI HERALD!

"Pretty middle name," I say
as I read Carmen's screen.

"It means 'harvest,' you know," she says.
Sound familiar, *Demetra?*"

My mouth opens.
Carmen looks smug.
"I knew we were going to be friends
from the beginning."

We FaceTime Ethan, too,
who has decided
to use guest interviewers for *The Scaled Fish*
and start a second podcast
investigating environmental news stories.
We brainstorm names together:
    The Endangered Fish?
    Green Island?
I like *Island Conservatory*,
but Ethan tells me
that's the name of *my* future podcast
about music.

Together
we get our presentation ready
for the town council.

IDENTITY CRISIS

Next on my list is piano.

This one is painful because
a pianist
is what I have been
since I was five.

Learning a new piece —
deciding which measures are my favorites,
hammering shape and feeling into the melodies
with my fingers,
conquering the sections
when the right and left hands
both turn into preposterous show-offs —
I still want all that.
But practicing more than two hours a day
and winning prizes
and even playing onstage at Carnegie Hall
just don't mean as much to me
as other things
right now.

My parents' faces,
overjoyed after my performances,
crowd my memories.

Lessons aren't cheap.
I feel a little
like an investment
about to become worthless . . .
like our old restaurant.

To me,
Say No to Plastic Bags on Wilford Island
is the Trident Restaurant.
A new opportunity in a new place.

I can't imagine that my mother
sees it that way.

ALTERNATIVE THINKING

In the spirit
of not doing it all by myself,
I text Lee
and tell her
that I might have to quit piano for a while.

QUIT?! she writes back.
WAIT, HOLD ON, I'M CALLING YOU.

On the phone,
she barely lets me speak.
"You were the one in Florida
talking all about the pleasures of performance,
or whatever that book was,
and how much you still love to play.
Think of how many kids hate piano
and still play it.
You love it!
You don't quit something you love!
Okay, skip the competition this year,
who cares,
but why does it have to be
all or nothing?"

Who cares . . .

Did my oldest friend
just point the way
for me?

I tell her I think she might be right,
and she tells me she knows she is,
and we talk more about the walkout.
I sent her as many photos from that day
as I did of beach shells
last July.

"You know what?"
Lee's voice turns into a throaty whisper.
"I told some people in chorus
that you got your whole middle school
to do a protest march,
and Michael asked
to see the pictures on my phone!
He thought it was cool —
it *is* really cool, Mimi.
Then he took a selfie
and handed the phone back,
but I said —
I still can't believe it —
'Wait, you forgot to put in your number
and choose a ringtone.'
And he did!"

My oldest friend's complete happiness
makes me smile.

OUT OF CURIOSITY

I ask Ms. Miller
when she started competing
in roller derby leagues,
and she said,
"Oh, not until I turned twenty.
I never even took
formal skating lessons
until I was an adult."

I don't ask if she had
passions
that were loud and sunny
when she was a kid,
and that got nudged to quieter,
shadier places
when she discovered roller derby,

because of course she did.

FERMATA

At my next lesson
I sit on the cushioned piano bench
clutching *The Pleasures of Piano Performance*
by R. Josefowitz.

My mother and Kyle
both wait
because I have said I want to tell them something . . .

but the music inside me
goes quiet.

Will my mother cry?
Or go silently furious?
Will Kyle say I can't
take lessons from him anymore
if I'm not serious about competing?

I try to summon words
for the requiem in my head.

In the silence,
my mother looks me
full in the face.
When she speaks, she sounds tired.

"I think what Mimi is trying to say
is that she wants
to withdraw from the competition this year."

STEPPING BACK

Kyle doesn't seem all that surprised.
I am quick to say
that I love him as a teacher,
but I just want to
cut back
to where playing and performing
bring me joy
and challenge me
and leave space for other things
I'm passionate about.

"What I'm hearing is
you're off-balance."
Kyle points a steady finger
at the book I'm still holding.
"Josefowitz says it.
Piano is a journey.
Everyone's is different."

He and my mother
discuss that we will continue lessons
through the spring.
Next fall will depend
on my commitment level,
but Kyle can recommend other local teachers

who would love to have me
as a student.

I'm uncomfortable
hearing this —
so, from the look of things,
is my mother —
but it still feels like
the best decision
for me
for now.

"All right. Let's get to it," Kyle says,
moving his chair next to my bench
and opening my music.
"Who better to bring joy
to your practice
than Chopin?"

RELUCTANT SUPPORT IS STILL SUPPORT

"It was all too much,"
my mother says
when she gets into the car
to fight Friday evening traffic
on the way home.
"Your life right now.
I see that.
You don't need to compete,
Demetra."

Her words don't match her face,
which still looks
as queasy
as if I'd announced I was going to
bungee off the causeway.

I can see she's trying,
and I'm grateful.

REGROWTH

My father wakes up
much earlier than normal
on Sunday.

From my bed,
I hear the car's tires
crunch over our shell driveway
when he leaves —
and when he returns.

"Loulouthi mou!"
He pokes his head into my room.
"How late are you going to sleep?"

I resist the urge
to toss my pillow at him.
Like my mom,
he was understanding when I told him
I was going to cut back on piano
because of my environmental work.
(He didn't have to
fake it as much, either.)

Once I get up
and pour a bowl of cereal,
I see where he went.

New vegetable plants
sit in pots next to the bare garden beds —
a bunch of leafy lettuces,
some cauliflower and broccoli,
onions, leeks, and garlic.

When I go outside,
he puts his arm around my shoulder.

"I refuse to believe
that you and I
can't grow vegetables here."
With his other arm
he gestures grandly at our scrubby yard.

"The bugs were pretty bad, Dad."

"Ah, but I have a little more time
now that the restaurant's on its feet," he replies.
"We'll battle those bugs together.
Demetra and Dad.
What do you say?"

We kneel down,
dig hollows in the dirt,
and nestle each plant in a cozy new home.

WHEN MY MOTHER SAID, "DRESS UP," I SHOULDN'T HAVE ROLLED MY EYES

The Wilford Island Town Hall
is a hurricane-safe building on stilts.

As I climb the twenty-two steps
to the front entrance,
I clutch the shoulder strap of my backpack,
which holds my speech
and my stainless-steel water bottle
in case my mouth goes dry.

I rehearsed last night
for today's
performance.

The January town council meeting
is a bunch of adults
in a low-ceilinged committee room
greeting one another and talking about
gutter repair
and orange juice muffin recipes

until the meeting begins.
Then, the reading of minutes,
the nominations and seconds,

and the "ayes" and "nays"
and "it is so ordereds"
make me sit up straighter
and be grateful that I wore
a pressed cardigan over my T-shirt
and some of Lee's eye shadow.

WE THE STUDENTS

When they arrive
at agenda item 7.a.,
Carmen leans into my side
and Ethan reaches for a quick low five.
I pat his hand
even though mine is clammy.

We stand
and each read part
of the speech we've prepared,

which begins
"We, the students of Wilford School,
who founded
Say No to Plastic Bags on Wilford Island,
believe . . ."

which repeats
the demands from the walkout,

which points out
that the island's largest food store,
Frank's,
has already committed
to using alternative bags,

which includes
passing our petition forward
so the five councilmembers —
four men and one woman —
can take a look.
The walkout and the news articles
helped us get to
four hundred sixty-four signatures.
Fewer than five hundred.
But still.

HOW LONG CAN THE EARTH WAIT?

When the five councilmembers
ask for community input,
the first person to jump to his feet
is Henry.

Deep-voiced once again,
he adjusts his glasses
and fumes
that it's a crying shame
that *children* have to be the ones
educating "the old folks"
(his words, not mine)
and pleading with elected representatives
to do the right thing
in this upside-down world.

The next speaker,
the owner of a tourist shop,
isn't on our side.

He says that he'll stop bagging in plastic
happily
if the town pays for it
or when the state of Florida
orders him to.

Otherwise, he's sorry,
but he can't afford to change.
And since the state is rolling back
local bans everywhere,
this petition is just a waste of time,
isn't it?

"Come on, man!"
Henry shouts.
"You're killing the earth
for your grandkids."

The shop owner actually
swears at Henry!

Some wildlife refuge members stand
and defend Henry,
and soon everyone is giving
one side or the other
a piece of their mind.

Councilmember Vaughan calls for order.

"Clearly," he says, "we are not prepared
to put any resolution
on this matter
to a vote today."

MOVING FORWARD

I swear I'll do it.
I'll howl and rage right here
in my take-me-seriously clothes.
The earth needs to heal —
to feel the relief of spring after a wrathful winter —
today,
not tomorrow.

Before my emotions erupt,
a grain of progress:

"Motion to create a task force,"
Councilmember Vaughan says,
"to assess costs and benefits
of supporting the community
in eliminating single-use plastic bags.
If the task force is efficient,
we can reconvene soon
to vote on our young friends' resolution,
which I, personally, find compelling."

"I second," the female councilmember says.
The motion carries.

"The council will entertain nominees
for the task force leader."

My hand shoots up
as if I'm in Ms. Miller's class
and she's asked us to name some places
where microplastics —
the tiny particles from plastic waste —
have been detected.
(Answers: Seafood. Honey. Beer.
Table salt. Tap water.
The air we breathe.
Unacceptable.)

I don't know if hand-raising
is part of council meetings,
but Councilmember Vaughan calls on me
just the same.

"I nominate Anne Lowell," I say.

PLEASE JOIN US ON JANUARY 18, 2020

We throw a party at our house,
to celebrate . . .

a.
the small victory
of the Single-Use Plastics Task Force,
which didn't exist
before we students petitioned islanders
and walked out of class,
and which Anne will hopefully lead
to a larger victory;

b.
my thirteenth birthday.

It was my mother's idea.
The Trident Restaurant catered.

Carmen was the first person I invited.

ISLAND PARTY

We clean for three days
and pack everyone into our tiny living room
with cups of white grape juice
(nonstaining)
and pastry plates.

Ms. Miller is standing by herself,
so I ask how Smaug is doing
and introduce her to
Anne and Henry
and their wildlife refuge friends.
I tell Anne that Ms. Miller is my favorite teacher
and a science teacher . . .
and could the task force
maybe use a science teacher?

"That one's
a natural community organizer,"
I hear Henry say
after I've walked away.

My lunch table friends
eat crumbling finikia pastries
and check out my garden.
I don't know if

the jaundiced broccoli
will make it,
but thanks to
my dad's fanatic morning inspections,
some of the lettuce greens are almost
ready to pick.

Carmen and her mother *and* father come!
Mr. Hill seems comfortable
being one of the heroes of our movement,
so I see no need to remind him
that we had to trick him into doing the right thing.

THE PLEASURES OF PIANO PERFORMANCE

I play a short set,
Chopin's Nocturne in F Major
and Chen Yi's Bamboo Dance II,
emotion-filled pieces
that Kyle and I have been
taking
slowly.

I try to bring awareness
to my body as I play,
the way Kyle taught me.
Although it's awkward
to perform in front of friends,
I do it because I am grateful
to everyone in my house,
and music is one of the gifts
I can give.

The adults applaud with evident delight.
Stephanie hugs me afterward,
and Ethan looks at me
as if, instead of playing,
I sprouted wings
and flew around the room.

"I can't — that was — I mean, I knew —
but — wow."

It gives me a little thrill
that music and I
made the boy,
who always has something to say,
lose his words.

THE TIDE MUST TURN

I find a quiet moment
to take Carmen and Ethan aside.

"What's next, Mimi?" asks Carmen.
"How are we going to help
the task force?"

"Anne says she's reallocated
town budgets before.
She'll try to find the money
to fund alternative bags
for the businesses that can't afford them.
Or raise it.
We've still got to work on
shifting the Wilford Island shopping culture
so that bringing reusables
becomes a habit.
But that's not all.
We have to start thinking big."

"How big?" asks Ethan.

I want to keep standing up.
Kids are angry at being handed
a suffering planet . . .

but there are a lot of us.
And, as Isabel reminded the adults
in that bowl-shaped auditorium,
"we are one hundred percent
of the future."

I grin at my friends' curious faces.
"Preemption law big."

CODA

EARTH CONCERTO

Even though I filled my glass vase
months ago,
I still slip shells into my pockets
on my taffy-sand beach.
I'm fussier now.
A junonia with a chipped end
doesn't make me stoop.
An unblemished whelk
still feels like treasure.

Rambling over the packed sand
helps me layer
the noisy ideas in my head
into buoyant, swelling harmonies.

My new movement
isn't played by a soloist
or a chamber orchestra.

It needs a mighty philharmonic.

SAY NO TO PLASTIC BAGS IN THE STATE OF FLORIDA

Kids in this state
are going to shape history.

We're forming
a *coalition* —
Ms. Miller's term —
to head to the Florida State Legislature
to lobby against
the preemption laws
that make it difficult
to ban plastic bags in our state.

Carmen's designing our website.
Ethan is investigating the laws
in his first-ever serialized podcast.
Stephanie's getting her school involved, too.
I send emails daily to student leaders,
introducing myself,
talking about single-use plastics,
telling Wilford Island's story,
asking kids I don't know
to tell theirs
and join us.

We want to clear the way
for a legal statewide ban.

And we plan to fight
like Melati and Isabel,

together,

until every last ghost

is gone.

AUTHOR'S NOTE

The environmental consequences of single-use plastic bags are devastating, but the tireless activism of Melati and Isabel Wijsen has brought light and hope. When Melati was twelve years old and Isabel just ten, the sisters founded Bye Bye Plastic Bags, a now global nonprofit organization, with the goal of making their island of Bali plastic bag–free. In 2014 the sisters convinced the governor of Bali to sign a commitment to ban plastic bags, and five years later this commitment became a reality when his successor enacted the ban.

Now, through a new venture, Youthtopia, Melati is sharing the lessons that she and Isabel have learned from their activism. With a team of changemakers, she is empowering young people worldwide to tackle an array of social and environmental causes.

In the novel, Mimi's story ends just as COVID-19 is beginning to cross the globe in the early months of 2020. I'd like to think that she, like the Wijsen sisters, would continue working remotely to implement her plastic bag boycott, to educate her community about the benefits of reusable bags, and to appeal to state lawmakers to repeal the restrictive preemption laws. As the sun sets on the pandemic, I imagine she would feel newly energized to continue the environmental work that is so desperately needed to cool the planet, repair damaged ecosystems, and preserve our species. Of course, we must all do this critical work together. Please see the next few pages for ways to get involved!

Wilford Island is fictitious, but it is based geographically on Sanibel Island, a verdant, stoplight-free vacation destination off the Gulf Coast of Florida. For the record, Sanibel, with its 6,400-acre wildlife refuge, is a model of environmental and ecological preservation. The general store on the island, Bailey's, no longer distributes single-use plastic bags, and Sanibel's nonprofit organization START launched a BYOB (Bring Your Own Bag) initiative in 2015.

Ecopoets and eco-justice poets have long illuminated uncomfortable truths about the climate crisis. While we must rely on science to develop urgent action plans, poetry connects us emotionally to the tragedy behind the statistics. This emotional potency is the reason I reached for the verse form when I set out to craft a story of environmental activism. My novel honors Melati and Isabel Wijsen and the other brave young activists who have confronted the plastic pollution problem and decided to fight back.

Thank you for joining Mimi on her journey. I wish you courage as you walk your own.

TIMELINE OF PLASTIC BAG ORIGINS, DISTRIBUTION, AND ACTIVISM

Early 1960s: The Swedish engineer Sten Gustaf Thulin invents the plastic "T-shirt bag," which earns its nickname from handles that give it the look of a sleeveless, scoop-neck shirt. Thulin envisions that plastic bags in circulation will be used not once, but stored and reused, eliminating the need to cut down trees for paper bags.

1965: The Swedish packaging company Celloplast patents the T-shirt bag and distributes it throughout Europe.

1982: Two of the biggest supermarket chains in the United States, Safeway and Kroger, begin distributing T-shirt bags. Within three years, plastic bags are offered alongside paper in seventy-five percent of American supermarkets.

1990s: Cheap to manufacture and transport, plastic bags replace paper bags in the majority of shops and stores around the world.

1997: While sailing from Hawaii to California, the oceanographer and boat captain Charles Moore discovers the Great Pacific Garbage Patch, a giant zone of plastic debris miles from land. Four more of these swirling gyres are identified in the earth's oceans in later years. Research reveals that plastic bags in the sea sink and become fragmented into smaller and smaller pieces known as *microplastics*. Aquatic animals ingest this toxic smog of plastic fragments, and they disturb seafloor ecosystems where they land.

2008: An estimated 500 billion to 1 trillion plastic bags are consumed worldwide. During the 2008 International Coastal Cleanup, plastic bags make up twelve percent of all garbage collected on the world's beaches. They are second only to cigarette butts. More than eighty percent of plastic bags end up in earth's landfills, where they may leach potentially toxic substances into the soil and water. Exposed to sunlight, plastic bags *photodegrade*, or break up into microscopic particles that never fully decompose. Deprived of sunlight, the bags may last, intact, centuries or more.

2013–2014: Twelve- and ten-year-old Melati and Isabel Wijsen launch Bye Bye Plastic Bags on Bali. They collect more than eighty-seven thousand petition signatures in support of a plastic bag ban on the island. They meet with local officials, create educational materials, and distribute alternative bags in a pilot village. Inspired by Gandhi, the sisters eventually go on a modified hunger strike, and within one day, Governor I Made Mangku Pastika agrees to meet with them. On camera, he signs an order banning plastic bags, plastic straws, and Styrofoam on the island by 2018.

2014: California becomes the first state in the United States to ban single-use plastic bags.

2016–2020: Though seven other states pass uniform statewide bag laws, twice as many state legislations preempt local plastic regulation on bags and containers, making bans and local ordinances difficult to legislate.

2018: Globally, more than one hundred sixty countries, regions, and cities enact legislation to ban plastic bags or charge a fee for their distribution. The Dutch inventor Boyan Slat deploys the ocean cleanup system he invented at age eighteen inside the Great Pacific Garbage Patch.

2019: After a lack of enforcement and accountability, the plastics ban on Bali finally takes effect under a new governor, I Wayan Koster.

2020–2021: The COVID-19 pandemic postpones or overturns regional plastic bag bans, as lawmakers fear that reusable bags will transmit the virus. Melati Wijsen founds Youthtopia, a project to train young changemakers and give them tools to make a difference. During the pandemic, Melati shares videos on how to be an activist from home.

Today: According to the EPA, 380 billion plastic bags and wraps are still used in the United States, requiring 12 million barrels of oil to create. After delays, bans are once again being enforced, and more cities, states, and countries worldwide are considering banning all single-use plastics.

TOMORROW

More young people are turning to environmental activism in the hopes
of making lasting change. Here are just a few examples of other
significant activists, some of whom are featured in this novel:

While in high school, **Karina Samuel** launched the Florida chapter of
Bye Bye Plastic Bags in 2019. She has raised more than ten thousand
dollars for the organization and coordinated more than thirty beach
cleanups throughout the state. Since the impacts of climate change
disproportionately affect low-income communities, Karina believes
that those capable of volunteering have a responsibility to do so for
others who can't.

The fifth-graders at P.S. 15 Patrick F. Daly School in Red Hook,
Brooklyn, New York, became citizen scientists and advocates for
reducing single-use plastics in their community and school. Working
with the environmental education organization Cafeteria Culture,
they testified and rallied at New York City Hall. Watch their journey
in the documentary *Microplastic Madness*.

Georgia resident **Hannah Testa** has been delivering presentations on
plastic pollution since the age of ten. As a high schooler in 2020, she
was one of a small group of advocates who introduced a federal bill,
the Break Free from Plastic Pollution Act, in Congress. She is the
author of *Taking On the Plastics Crisis*.

Autumn Peltier, Anishinaabe-kwe, from the Wiikwemkoong First Nation on Manitoulin Island in Ontario, Canada, is a water activist. When she was twelve, at the Assembly of First Nations, she confronted Prime Minister Justin Trudeau about the Canadian oil pipelines, to which he replied, "I will protect the water." She has spoken to the United Nations and has called for a plastics ban and a return to more sustainable ways of life.

At sixteen, **Isra Hirsi** served as the cofounder and co–executive director of the U.S. Youth Climate Strike, a multiday gathering of speakers and organizers in Washington, D.C. The daughter of Minnesota congresswoman Ilhan Omar, Isra speaks against environmental racism and works to help those who are disproportionately affected by climate change to advocate for themselves and their communities.

Greta Thunberg considered our planet's climate emergency so dire that she left school in ninth grade to strike, alone, in front of the Swedish Parliament building. Her singular boldness inspired millions around the globe to join the fight. She has met with world leaders and continues to push for aggressive green legislation and to illuminate the intersection between racial and climate justice.

GET INVOLVED

LEARN more about the Wijsen sisters and JOIN their global team of activists!

Watch Melati and Isabel's TED Talk:

Wijsen, Isabel and Melati Wijsen. "Our Campaign to Ban Plastic Bags in Bali." *TEDGlobal>London*. September 2015. ted.com/talks/melati_and _isabel_wijsen_our_campaign_to_ban_plastic_bags_in_bali.

Start a new Bye Bye Plastic Bags team or join one in your region:

At the time of this printing, there are U.S. teams in California, Florida, New Jersey, New York, North Carolina, and Pennsylvania. To join a Bye Bye Plastic Bags team or to start your own, visit byebyeplasticbags.org.

Follow Youthtopia and learn about how to organize:

Instagram: @youthtopia.world

Twitter: @youthtopiaworld

YouTube Channel: YOUTHTOPIA

Facebook: facebook.com/YOUTHTOPIA.world

ENGAGE with other youth-oriented environmental activism organizations!

Jane Goodall's Roots & Shoots

Roots & Shoots is a global movement of young people who are empowered to use their voices and actions to make compassionate decisions, influencing and leading change in their communities.

rootsandshoots.org

Oceana

As a policy-oriented ocean conservation organization, Oceana is focused on passing legislation on the local, state, and federal level that preserves and protects our blue planet. Sailors for the Sea, a project of Oceana, offers Kids Environmental Lesson Plans (KELP) that encourage children's curiosity about all things marine, including plastic. Oceana's international site houses a *Marine Life Encyclopedia* for both kids and adults.

usa.oceana.org/plastics

sailorsforthesea.org/programs/kelp

5 Gyres: Science to Solutions

Through science, art, education, and adventure, 5 Gyres empowers action against the global health crisis of plastic pollution. You can learn more about plastics by watching their Trash Academy videos.

5gyres.org

Surfrider Foundation

Dedicated to the protection and enjoyment of the world's oceans, waves, and beaches, Surfrider's Student Club Network offers opportunities for young people to influence environmental action through service, leadership development, civic engagement, and direct action organizing.

surfrider.org

National Geographic Kids: Kids vs. Plastic

National Geographic Kids is a children's magazine published by the National Geographic Society. Help fight pollution with downloadable tool kits and tips on how to live a plastic-free life.

kids.nationalgeographic.com/explore/nature/kids-vs-plastic

READ about plastic waste and environmental activism!

Burns, Loree Griffin. *Tracking Trash: Flotsam, Jetsam, and the Science of Ocean Motion*. Boston: HMH Books for Young Readers, reprint edition, 2010.

Clinton, Chelsea. *Start Now! You Can Make a Difference*. New York: Philomel Books, 2018.

Eamer, Claire. *What a Waste: Where Does Garbage Go?* Illus. by Bambi Edlund. Toronto: Annick Press, 2017.

Newman, Patricia. *Plastic, Ahoy! Investigating the Great Pacific Garbage Patch*. Minneapolis: Millbrook Press, 2014.

Testa, Hannah. *Taking On the Plastics Crisis*. New York: Penguin Workshop, 2020.

Thunberg, Greta. *No One Is Too Small to Make a Big Difference*. New York: Penguin Books, 2019.

ACT locally with Cafeteria Culture's Recipe for #plasticfree Change!

Visit cafeteriaculture.org for information on how to conduct a simple one-week home **waste audit**. Cafeteria Culture works creatively with youth to achieve zero-waste, climate-smart communities and a plastic-free biosphere. The following steps are adapted from their Recipe for #plasticfree Change.

To start:

+ Save all your single-use plastic packaging for one week.
+ Lay it all out on a tarp or old sheet and organize the items by the following categories:
    1. **Personal/Home:** items you have control over and can reduce simply by refusing to purchase
    2. **Local Shopping:** single-use plastics that are routinely included with your to-go food or retail store purchases, such as plastic bags, straws, cutlery, and access packaging
    3. **Manufacturers:** single-use plastic packaging used for shipping, and as part of the design of containers, and excessive, nonrecyclable plastic wrapping of produce, snack foods, clothing, and electronics
+ Photograph the items as arranged. You may want to share your photos with stores, manufacturers, and policy makers as visual data or post them to social media.

Then, take action:

Youth-led action is urgently needed for system-wide **policy** changes. Schools' food policies can eliminate single-use plastics. Well-crafted local, state, and national laws can also stop plastic pollution "upstream" and lead to long-lasting change. Call, write, or ask to meet with your local representatives!

Find the full Recipe for #plasticfree Change and many more action ideas at www.cafeteriaculture.org/recipe-for-plasticfree-change.html.

HEAR from a scientist on the front lines of plastic pollution research!

The environmental scientist, educator, and author **Dr. Marcus Eriksen** cofounded the 5 Gyres Institute to research plastic pollution in the world's oceans, and he recently cofounded Leap Lab, a network of science centers committed to building self-reliant communities. He answers questions about his work and explains the way a single person willing to organize can make change happen.

You have sailed through all five subtropical ocean gyres on research expeditions. Could you give an example of encountering plastic garbage in the ocean?

Crossing a gyre, it's easy to see microplastic when the wind slows down. On some days, the wind stopped completely and the ocean became flat, revealing a kaleidoscope of plastic particles, like constellations in the night sky. But also at night, you can watch myctophid fish eating microplastics as they forage on the ocean surface. Myctophid fish make up one-sixth of the ocean's biomass of fish. They are eating our trash.

I've seen large macroplastic items in the ocean, from upside-down boats to massive multiton balls of tangled fishing nets and line. One five-hundred-pound net bolus was lifted out of the ocean and onto our boat. I shook it, and fifty starfish fell out, along with dozens of fish, worms, and snails. It was an ecosystem living on waste. I also found three dead fish in the net, which had been there awhile. It showed me that lost fishing nets don't stop fishing. A lost fishing net can kill more fish when lost than when it's used by a fisherman.

What are some ecological impacts of plastic waste that you've witnessed or studied?

It's common to find wildlife in the ocean using plastic to live on, or live in. I have found fish, crabs, and snails living in massive floating nets, sometimes entangled. I have found fish with their stomachs filled with plastic waste. I've seen marine mammals and sea turtles with their limbs — and sometimes their heads — strangled in old fishing nets, packing straps, or ropes.

What about on land?

I recently published a paper about camels eating plastic bags. Its purpose is largely to show that the issue of plastic pollution is just as devastating on land as it is in the ocean.

You talk about zero-waste communities in your book *Junk Raft: An Ocean Voyage and a Rising Tide of Activism to Fight Plastic Pollution*. What steps might someone take to make their community a zero-waste community?

Organize, organize, organize! We must organize in our communities to identify the systems that are creating waste. Maybe it's a lack of food scrap sorting and collection, or a lack of recycling centers to bring aluminum cans to. Maybe it's a lack of reusable systems, like dishwashing in schools or big government and corporate procurement departments buying lots of single-use throwaway items. Whatever it is, wherever you start, get organized, get strategic, and take on the most wasteful systems one at a time.

Find out more about Dr. Eriksen at marcuseriksen.com.

ACKNOWLEDGMENTS

I am grateful to the following readers and experts for help with the environmental, musical, learning disability, and other narrative content in this novel. You touched Mimi's story indelibly:

 Jeannine Atkins

 Tanya Auger

 Tiffany Hays Borsch

 Debby Lee Cohen

 Marcus Eriksen, PhD

 Cindy Genevieve Giron

 Lorelei Kuan

 Kate McGovern

 Atsuko Quirk

 Astrid Rapoza

 Zaidee B. Rose

 Kimberly Warner, PhD

 Bethany Vinhateiro, #earthgoddess, this novel is your brainchild, and I thank you for entrusting it to me and for nurturing it with your greenest of editorial thumbs as it took root. Thank you to Whitney Leader-Picone for your graceful and inviting book design that honors the verse form. Dana Sanmar, your triumphant cover dynamically captures Mimi's spirit and the power of collaborative activism. Huge thanks to my tireless publishing team, including Maxine Bartow,

Sammy Brown, Susan Buckheit, Zoe Del Mar, Emma Grant, Mary Magrisso, Margaret Rosewitz, and Erika West. Allison Hellegers, you guide my writing journey with wisdom, tenacity, and warmth. I am fortunate to have you at my helm.

Thank you to Dimitri, Gail, and Tom Dimopoulos and to John and Dorothy Evans, for both the novel's cultural texture and the family vacations to Florida that inspired its setting. Thank you, as well, to the Simmons University children's literature community, which has nourished my creativity for so many years. I am grateful from afar to my novelist- and memoirist-in-verse idols, Helen Frost, Nikki Grimes, and Karen Hesse. Read their books!

Nicholas, Athena, and John Evans, you are my significant people. Just when I think my heart can't swell with any more love for you, the sun rises on a new day.

Finally, deepest gratitude to the incredible Wijsen sisters, Melati and Isabel. Keep spreading the light of youth activism throughout the world.

SELECTED BIBLIOGRAPHY

ARTICLES

"First Step" (40)

Ingram, Julia. "Cities Are Stymied in Banning Plastics — and the State Is Doing Nothing About It, They Say." *Miami Herald*. August 22, 2019. miamiherald.com/news/local/environment/article234158642.html.

"Preemption Laws." *PlasticBagLaws.org*. July 22, 2020. plasticbaglaws.org /preemption.

"A Grainy Underwater Photograph" (50)

Gibbens, Sarah. "Plastic Proliferates at the Bottom of World's Deepest Ocean Trench." *National Geographic.com*. May 13, 2019. nationalgeographic.com/science/article/plastic-bag-mariana-trench -pollution-science-spd.

Morrelle, Rebecca. "Mariana Trench: Deepest-Ever Sub Dive Finds Plastic Bag." *bbc.com*. British Broadcasting Corporation. May 13, 2019. bbc .com/news/science-environment-48230157.

"The Age of Plastic" (52)

Menicagli, Virginia, Elena Balestri, and Claudio Lardicci. "Exposure of Coastal Dune Vegetation to Plastic Bag Leachates: A Neglected Impact of Plastic Litter." *Science of the Total Environment* 683 (September 15, 2019): 737–48.

Rochman, Chelsea M., B. Halpern, Mark Anthony Browne, Benjamin S. Halpern, Brian T. Hentschel, Eunha Hoh, Hrissi K. Karapanagioti,

Lorena M. Rios-Mendoza, Hideshige Takada, Swee Teh, and Richard C. Thompson. "Classify Plastic Waste as Hazardous." *Nature* 494 (February 13, 2013): 169–71.

Shiver, Jube, Jr. "Battle of the Bags: Paper or Plastic?" *LATimes.com*. *Los Angeles Times*. June 13, 1986. latimes.com/archives/la-xpm-1986-06 -13-mn-10728-story.html.

Ward, Collin P., and Christopher M. Reddy. "We Need Better Data About the Environmental Persistence of Plastic Goods." *Proceedings of the National Academy of Sciences of the United States of America (PNAS)* 117, no. 26 (June 30, 2020): 14618–21.

"The Greek Myth of Arion and the Dolphins Leaps to My Mind" (67)

Alesali, Loumay, and Justin Lear. "Stranded Baby Dolphin in Florida Had Plastic Trash in Its Stomach." *CNN.com*. Cable News Network. April 29, 2019. cnn.com/2019/04/29/us/rough-toothed-dolphin -stranded/index.html.

"The New Plastics Economy: Rethinking the Future of Plastics." Report by Project Mainstream, developed by the World Economic Forum and the Ellen MacArthur Foundation, with McKinsey & Company as knowledge partner. January 19, 2016. ellenmacarthurfoundation .org/publications/the-new-plastics-economy-rethinking-the-future -of-plastics.

"Stealing from Melati and Isabel's Playbook" (70)

Davis, Karen. "From Bali to the World's Stage: Meet Melati and Isabel Wijsen." *Indonesia Expat*. July 26, 2016. indonesiaexpat.id/meet-the -expats/from-bali-to-the-worlds-stage-meet-melati-and-isabel-wijsen.

"Significant Lunch: A Daydream" (82)

"Greta Thunberg: Who Is She and What Does She Want?" *BBC.com*.
British Broadcasting Company. February 28, 2020. bbc.com/news
/world-europe-49918719.

Hirsi, Isra. "The Climate Movement Needs More People Like Me." *Grist*.
March 25, 2019. grist.org/article/the-climate-movement-needs-more
-people-like-me.

Riggio, Olivia. "Autumn Peltier: 'Water Warrior' for Marginalized Communities." *KCET.org*. September 16, 2020. kcet.org/shows/tending
-nature/autumn-peltier-water-warrior-for-marginalized-communities.

"Eutrophication" (109)

"Hurricane Dorian Brings Chunks of Red Drift Algae to Sanibel Island."
September 4, 2019. *WinkNews.com*. winknews.com/2019/09/04
/hurricane-dorian-brings-chunks-of-red-drift-algae-to-sanibel-island.

Mansell, Crystal. "Hurricane Dorian Status Update #1." *MySanibel.com*.
August 29, 2019. mysanibel.com/Departments/City-Manager-s
-Office/News/HURRICANE-DORIAN-STATUS-UPDATE-1-8
-29-2019-9-a.m.

"More Dorians" (111)

Bauman, Brooke. "How Plastics Contribute to Climate Change." *Yale
Climate Connections*. August 20, 2019. yaleclimateconnections.org
/2019/08/how-plastics-contribute-to-climate-change.

Sabella, Giuseppe. "Climate Change Puts Florida at Risk. Public Schools
Are Not Teaching It the Right Way, Experts Say." *WLRN.org*. November 11, 2019. wlrn.org/environment/2019-11-11/climate-change

-puts-florida-at-risk-public-schools-are-not-teaching-it-the-right-way
-experts-say.

"Waste" (112)

Katz, Brigit. "Do 'Biodegradable' Plastic Bags Actually Degrade?" *Smithsonian Magazine*. May 1, 2019. smithsonianmag.com/smart-news/do
-biodegradable-plastic-bags-actually-biodegrade-180972074.

Tineo, Andrea. "Trying to Recycle That Plastic Bag? The Odds Are
Nine to One It's Not Happening." *Ecology Center*. January 27, 2020.
ecologycenter.org/blog/trying-to-recycle-that-plastic-bag-the-odds
-are-nine-to-one-its-not-happening.

"Insincere" (151)

Stein, Vicky. "How Biodegradable Plastic Bags Don't Live Up to Their
Name." *PBS.org*. *PBS NewsHour*. May 2, 2019. pbs.org/newshour
/science/how-biodegradable-plastic-bags-dont-live-up-to-their-name.

"The Dirty Truth" (155)

Muthia, Risyiana. "Bali Ban on Single-Use Plastics Widely Ignored by
Small Businesses on Holiday Island — 'My Customers Expect Plastic
Bags.'" *South China Morning Post*. November 12, 2019. scmp.com
/lifestyle/travel-leisure/article/3036927/bali-ban-single-use-plastics
-widely-ignored-small.

"The Dirtier Truth" (157)

Cho, Renee. "Plastic, Paper, or Cotton: Which Shopping Bag Is Best?"
From the series Sustainable Living. *State of the Planet*, The Earth

Institute, Columbia University. April 30, 2020. blogs.ei.columbia.edu
/2020/04/30/plastic-paper-cotton-bags.

Chrobak, Ula. "Plastic Bags Are Still Bad for the Environment, Despite
Misleading Reports." *Popular Science.* June 14, 2019. www.popsci
.com/plastic-bag-better-than-reusable-tote.

Dillon, Noah. "Are Tote Bags Really Good for the Environment?" *The Atlantic.* September 2, 2016. theatlantic.com/technology/archive/2016
/09/to-tote-or-note-to-tote/498557.

Plumer, Brad. "Plastic Bags, or Paper? Here's What to Consider When
You Hit the Grocery Store." *Nytimes.com. New York Times.* March
29, 2019. nytimes.com/2019/03/29/climate/plastic-paper-shopping
-bags.html.

"RIP @WIPlasticBagBoycott" (215)

Weise, Elizabeth. "Online Haters Are Targeting Greta Thunberg with
Conspiracy Theories and Fake Photos." *USA Today.* October 2, 2019.
usatoday.com/story/news/nation/2019/10/02/climate-change
-activist-greta-thunberg-targeted-online-trolls/3843196002.

"Moving Forward" (321)

Rogers, Kara. "Microplastics." *Encyclopedia Britannica.* August 20, 2020.
britannica.com/technology/microplastic.

Schwartz, John. "Where's Airborne Plastic? Everywhere, Scientists Find."
New York Times. June 11, 2020. nytimes.com/2020/06/11/climate
/airborne-plastic-pollution.html.

Author's Note (334)

Paddock, Richard C. "After Fighting Plastic in 'Paradise Lost,' Sisters Take
On Climate Change." The Saturday Profile, *New York Times*. July
3, 2020. nytimes.com/2020/07/03/world/asia/bali-sisters-plastic
-climate-change.html.

"Sanibel STARTing to Phase Out Plastic Bags." *Captivasanibel.com*.
Sanibel Captiva Island Reporter, Islander & Current. December 2,
2015. captivasanibel.com/2015/12/02/sanibel-starting-to-phase-out
-plastic-bags.

Timeline of Plastic Bag Origins . . . (336)

Anderson, Marcia. "Confronting Plastic Pollution One Bag at a Time." *The
EPA Blog*. Environmental Protection Agency. November 1, 2016. blog
.epa.gov/2016/11/01/confronting-plastic-pollution-one-bag-at-a
-time.

"California Proposition 67, Plastic Bag Ban Veto Referendum (2016)."
Ballotpedia. ballotpedia.org/California_Proposition_67,_Plastic_Bag
_Ban_Veto_Referendum_(2016).

Chappell, Bill. "Ban on Single-Use Plastics Is Enacted in California." *NPR
.org*. National Public Radio. September 30, 2014. npr.org/sections
/thetwo-way/2014/09/30/352774915/ban-on-single-use-plastic
-bags-is-enacted-in-california.

Kerns, Sabrina. "Local Young Activist Releases New Book on Her Journey
to Creating Change for the Environment." *Forsyth County News*.
October 19, 2020. forsythnews.com/life/people/local-young-activist
-releases-new-book-her-journey-creating-change-environment.

Laskow, Sarah. "How the Plastic Bag Became So Popular." *The Atlantic*.

October 10, 2014. theatlantic.com/technology/archive/2014/10
/how-the-plastic-bag-became-so-popular/381065.

Petru, Alexis. "A Brief History of the Plastic Bag." *TriplePundit.com.* November 5, 2014. triplepundit.com/story/2014/brief-history-plastic
-bag/39406.

"A Rising Tide of Ocean Debris and What We Can Do About It." *Ocean Conservancy.* 2009 Report, International Coastal Cleanup, March 10, 2009. oceanconservancy.org/wp-content/uploads/2017/04/2009
-Ocean-Conservancy-ICC-Report.pdf.

"Saying 'Bye Bye' to Plastic Pollution, Teen Volunteers to Help Underserved Communities." *PointsofLight.org.* Daily Point of Light #6826, July 23, 2020. pointsoflight.org/awards/saying-bye-bye-to-plastic
-pollution-teen-volunteers-to-help-underserved-communities.

"State Plastic Bag Legislation." *National Conference of State Legislatures.* November 18, 2020. ncsl.org/research/environment-and-natural
-resources/plastic-bag-legislation.aspx.

Weston, Phoebe. "Plastic Bags Were Created to Save the Planet, Inventor's Son Says." *Independent.com. The Independent.* October 17, 2019. independent.co.uk/environment/plastic-bags-pollution-paper-cotton
-tote-bags-environment-a9159731.html.

HEAR from a scientist . . . (347)

Eriksen, Marcus, Amy Lusher, Mia Nixon, and Ulrich Wernery. "The Plight of Camels Eating Plastic Waste." *Journal of Arid Environments* 185 (February 2021): 1–6.

BOOKS

Abbing, Michiel Roscam. *Plastic Soup: An Atlas of Ocean Pollution*. Washington, D.C.: Island Press, 2019.

Eriksen, Marcus. *Junk Raft: An Ocean Voyage and a Rising Tide of Activism to Fight Plastic Pollution*. Boston: Beacon Press, 2017.

Freinkel, Susan. *Plastic: A Toxic Love Story*. Boston: Houghton Mifflin Harcourt, 2011.

McCallum, Will. *How to Give Up Plastic: A Guide to Changing the World, One Plastic Bottle at a Time*. London: Penguin Books, 2018.

Moore, Capt. Charles, with Cassandra Phillips. *Plastic Ocean*. New York: Avery, 2011.

Royte, Elizabeth. *Garbage Land: On the Secret Trail of Trash*. New York: Little, Brown and Company, 2005.

ADDITIONAL WEBSITES

5 Gyres: 5gyres.org

American Chemistry Council: americanchemistry.com

American Recyclable Plastic Bag Alliance: bagalliance.org

Break Free from Plastic: breakfreefromplastic.org

Bye Bye Plastic Bags: byebyeplasticbags.org

Cafeteria Culture: cafeteriaculture.org

Ellen MacArthur Foundation: ellenmacarthurfoundation.org

Leap Lab: leaplab.org

The Ocean Cleanup: theoceancleanup.com

Oceana: usa.oceana.org/plastics

Plastic Smart Cities: plasticsmartcities.org

PlasticBagLaws.org: plasticbaglaws.org

Plastics Industry Association: plasticsindustry.org

Surfrider Foundation: surfrider.org

World Wildlife Fund: worldwildlife.org

LECTURES AND PODCASTS

Cohen, Debby Lee, and Atsuko Quirk, panelists. Panel discussion. *Live Q&A with* Microplastic Madness's *Directors.* Belmont World Film's 18th Annual Family Festival, Virtual Edition. January 23, 2021.

Forbes, Megan, host. "Garbage Patches: How Gyres Take Our Trash Out to Sea." *NOAA Ocean Podcast.* National Ocean Service, Episode March 14, 2018. oceanservice.noaa.gov/podcast/mar18/nop14-ocean -garbage-patches.html.

Jones, Van. "The Economic Injustice of Plastic." *TEDxGreatPacific GarbagePatch.* November 2010, ted.com/talks/van_jones_the _economic_injustice_of_plastic#t-672327.

Wijsen, Isabel and Melati Wijsen. "Our Campaign to Ban Plastic Bags in Bali." *TedGlobal>London.* September 2015. ted.com/talks/melati_and _isabel_wijsen_our_campaign_to_ban_plastic_bags_in_bali.

Wijsen, Melati and Isabel Wijsen. "Melati and Isabel Wijsen — World Oceans Day 2017." *UN.org.* June 9, 2017. un.org/sustainablede velopment/blog/2017/06/melati-and-isabel-wijsen-world-oceans -day-2017.

FILM

Microplastic Madness. Directed and produced by Atsuko Quirk and Debby Lee Cohen. A Cafeteria Culture Production, 2019.